"I just wanted to say—"

Janie hesitated, like she was treading on uncertain ground.

"I don't want to talk about it," he said.

"You don't even know what I was going to say."

The hurt in her voice twisted in his stomach. They had to be missing something. He couldn't believe that Janie was guilty.

"I'm sorry," he said. "I know I said I'd do better about accepting praise for my work, but I'm tired and it's been a long day."

She reached over and touched his arm. "I understand. But that's not entirely what I wanted to talk about. I mean yes, what you've been doing here is a big deal. But I feel bad that you came here for one purpose, and you spent so little time with your family. It must be frustrating for you not to get to know them because you're spending all your time helping me."

Except that he was fulfilling his purpose. That's the part she missed. The part he couldn't tell her.

Danica Favorite loves the adventure of living a creative life. She loves to explore the depths of human nature and follow people on the journey to happily-ever-after. Though the journey is often bumpy, those bumps refine imperfect characters as they live the life God created them for. Oops, that just spoiled the ending of Danica's stories. Then again, getting there is all the fun. Find her at danicafavorite.com.

Books by Danica Favorite

Love Inspired

Double R Legacy

The Cowboy's Sacrifice
His True Purpose

Three Sisters Ranch

Her Cowboy Inheritance
The Cowboy's Faith
His Christmas Redemption

Love Inspired Historical

Rocky Mountain Dreams
The Lawman's Redemption
Shotgun Marriage
The Nanny's Little Matchmakers
For the Sake of the Children
An Unlikely Mother
Mistletoe Mommy
Honor-Bound Lawman

Visit the Author Profile page at Harlequin.com for more titles.

His True Purpose

Danica Favorite

LOVE INSPIRED
INSPIRATIONAL ROMANCE

LOVE INSPIRED®
INSPIRATIONAL ROMANCE

Recycling programs
for this product may
not exist in your area.

ISBN-13: 978-1-335-55385-0

His True Purpose

Copyright © 2020 by Danica Favorite

All rights reserved. No part of this book may be used or reproduced in
any manner whatsoever without written permission except in the case of
brief quotations embodied in critical articles and reviews.

This is a work of fiction. Names, characters, places and incidents are either the
product of the author's imagination or are used fictitiously. Any resemblance
to actual persons, living or dead, businesses, companies, events or locales is
entirely coincidental.

This edition published by arrangement with Harlequin Books S.A.

For questions and comments about the quality of this book,
please contact us at CustomerService@Harlequin.com.

Love Inspired
22 Adelaide St. West, 40th Floor
Toronto, Ontario M5H 4E3, Canada
www.Harlequin.com

Printed in U.S.A.

But as for you, ye thought evil against me;
but God meant it unto good, to bring to pass,
as it is this day, to save much people alive.
—*Genesis* 50:20

For the real Shelley and the real bunco group. You have all taught me so much about friendship and what it means to be there for one another through thick and thin. Thank you, ladies, for sharing your lives with me.

Chapter One

The same white car passed the church for the third time, driving at a snail's pace. Janie Roberts didn't recognize the car, so as it inched past, she took a look at the license plate. The red-and-white colors meant it was likely a rental.

Her mother's funeral service had concluded over an hour ago, and the receiving line had just wrapped up. Anyone who intended to be at the funeral should be inside already, but Janie supposed that a latecomer from out of town could be just arriving. But why would they be circling the building rather than finding a place to park and going inside?

The sheriff had warned them that criminals sometimes rob a recently deceased person's house during the funeral. But they had people watching both her father's house and Janie's.

So why did she feel so uneasy?

Janie took a deep breath. Probably because of that creepy investigator who'd come by her house a couple of weeks ago, asking her questions about her son, Sam, then demanding she sign a nondisclosure agreement, promising to never reveal the identity of Sam's father and her relationship with him. He'd offered her money, but it had felt wrong, considering she hadn't ever told anyone about Sam's father. He'd never given Janie a dime, and though she had been initially resentful of his absence, it had become a source of pride that she'd been able to do it all on her own.

Plus, Janie had known her mother's end was near, and she didn't want to dredge up the past she'd so firmly buried.

The man had finally left, but ever since then, Janie had felt an uneasy feeling, like someone was watching them.

Was he back?

The car turned the corner again, leaving Janie to her solitude.

The prayer garden at the Columbine Springs Community Church was a welcome respite from the activity going on in the building. She should have been inside, listening to all the well-wishers tell her how sorry they were for the loss of her mother. But she didn't want any of the sympathy.

Janie knew all these things, but talking about it wasn't going to make it better, or bring her mother back.

What she wanted was to do something useful. To feel normal.

She'd been trying, but Allison McNabb had literally taken the coffeepot out of her hands when Janie was refilling it. Yes, Janie knew this was her mother's funeral and she was supposed to be the one being comforted. But why couldn't people understand that for her, the act of brewing a pot of coffee, something she did countless times a day, was comforting.

Janie looked around the garden and took a deep breath. The roses had lost their buds and leaves weeks ago, and the thorny branches were a stark reminder of her loss. Maybe Mother Nature knew that Janie would be losing her own mother, and the bleak garden mourned the loss of the woman who had tenderly planted every single rosebush.

She glanced over at the church. She should probably go back in, but she couldn't stomach the idea of being told by anyone else how she should feel. Why couldn't people let her grieve her mother in her way? Janie was certain that if one more person tried to shove a plate of food into her hands and tell her to eat, she just might throw up. Food wasn't what Janie wanted.

She wanted the comfort of her mother's arms, and more importantly, she needed to hear her mother's wisdom.

Janie might have been caring for her dying mother, but the school had just sent her a letter saying that her request for reading therapy for her son, Sam, had been denied. Sam was at the top of the bottom when it came to reading scores, and, therefore, he didn't qualify for any extra help. Janie had looked into hiring a private reading specialist to help him, but it was so expensive, she didn't know how she would afford it. It wasn't that she was going to ask her mother for the money— her parents had already done so much for her and Sam.

But she knew her mother would have some advice on what steps to take next.

They said bad news came in threes, and in Janie's case, that was certainly true. Two days before Janie's mother died, the community resource center where she worked part-time had received notification from one of its biggest donors that they would be unable to continue paying for the grant that had been helping support the center since its opening. The center had a month's worth of funding, and then they were going to have to significantly reduce hours and services for a community that so desperately needed it.

Yes, the part-time job gave Janie some extra money, but it wasn't just about Janie's finances. She still had her full-time job at the elementary school as a teacher's aide, and it covered their basic needs. But for all the extras? She'd find something. Hopefully, a big something, since she'd have to replace that income plus find extra to help her son.

Maybe Janie should've taken that creepy investigator's offer. The amount of money had seemed like an awful lot, and when she hesitated, he'd asked her to name her number.

Another part of her thought it wasn't fair to Sam. At seven, he was obsessed with the idea of knowing who his dad was and having his own. Especially since his friend Katie had recently gotten a dad. Before that, his friend Ryan had gotten a new dad. Finding one for Sam now meant that Janie would have to get out there and date, and she wasn't willing to risk getting her heart broken again.

When Sam was old enough, he deserved to know who his father was and do what he wanted with that information, whether it be to find him or to write him off the way he'd been written off his whole life. Even now, feeling the financial pressure, she didn't think she could feel good about herself, looking her son in the eye and telling him she'd signed away his right to know for a bunch of lousy money.

She would give just about anything to hear what her mother had to say on the matter.

Tears rolled down her cheeks as Janie sat in her mother's favorite place in the whole world, feeling completely disconnected from the woman who'd always been there for her.

Yes, Janie had friends, but right now, she just wanted her mom.

Her mother was gone before Janie could ask all the questions she wanted, say all the things she needed, and while her mother had done an excellent job of preparing them all for this end, making her wishes known, the advice she hadn't given Janie was how to live without her.

If she asked her mother, she'd probably tell Janie to pray about it, but Janie didn't know what to pray for. A pastor's daughter, she'd been going to church her whole life, and she had no idea what to say to Him right now.

Janie glanced over at the small statue of

Jesus at the corner of the garden, inviting people to give their burdens to Him.

She knew that He knew what she needed, and all things would work out for the glory of God, but right now, she wasn't sure how. She couldn't imagine it would come in the form of poorly brewed coffee and feeling utterly helpless.

The same car she'd been observing slowed in front of the church again.

Whoever it was was obviously lost, or maybe felt some uncertainty about coming late to her mother's funeral. Also, there didn't look to be any available parking for several blocks.

At least this was an area where she could finally be useful. Janie took a deep breath and walked over to the car.

As she approached, the driver slowed to a stop and rolled down the window.

"Hi," Janie said. "Are you here for the funeral?"

The man shook his head. Something about him called to her, though she couldn't say why. He had an air about him that spoke of deep sadness. Maybe he was some long-lost relative or friend that Janie didn't know about.

"I needed to talk to a pastor," he said. "But I'm not going to interrupt a funeral. I'm just trying to figure out what to do in the meantime. I passed the café coming to town, but it looks closed."

That explained why the man called to her. He needed help, and she always seemed to find herself pulled toward people who needed her.

"I'm sorry to disappoint you," she said. "But you're going to find that everything in town is closed today. Everyone is at the funeral."

He looked skeptical. "Everyone? What about people's businesses? Surely they have someone staying behind."

Janie shook her head. "We're a small town. When one of our own passes, we all mourn."

He gave her a funny look, like he couldn't comprehend the entire town caring about someone enough to close everything to say goodbye.

"What about you? Why aren't you in there?" he asked.

Janie shrugged. "The funeral is over. Everyone is gathering in the fellowship hall, and I needed some air."

And something to do so she didn't feel useless. This was why she had to believe that perhaps God had sent this man her way because He understood how desperately Janie needed to feel useful and do something, rather than letting everyone else wait on her hand and foot.

"You could join us," Janie offered. "I'm sure there's plenty of food, because everyone overcooks, trying to outdo one another. It's as if they think their sorrow can be measured in the number of ham sandwiches and potato casseroles they make."

The man looked taken aback. "I wouldn't want to intrude. I don't know anyone here."

Her mother would insist he join them. And if he refused, she'd bring him a plate of food and encourage him to share his troubles.

"Yes, but the woman who died believed in showing kindness to strangers. She would have been the first to invite you in."

"I could use a cup of coffee," the man said slowly. "But I wouldn't feel right going in there."

Janie looked over at where her car was parked in the overflow lot, then turned back to him. "See that blue car? That's mine. If you park behind me, the only person you're blocking in is me, and I'm not leaving anytime soon. Park there, and meet me back here. I'll get us some coffee."

For a moment, she thought the man was going to say no. But then he nodded slowly. "All right."

She shouldn't have felt such satisfaction

at his agreement, but as she walked back to the church, watching as the man drove to the spot she'd indicated, Janie couldn't help feeling like God had answered her prayer. And maybe, just maybe, she could find a sense of normalcy without her mother.

Crashing an old lady's funeral wasn't part of Alexander Bennett's job description. In his defense, he hadn't known a funeral would be going on when he'd planned this trip.

Worse, the woman whose life was being celebrated wasn't just a random woman. She was the mother of the woman he was searching for.

Bad timing, but it couldn't be helped.

He had a job to do: find Janie Roberts, discover her sentiment toward State Senator James Blackwell, and then get her to sign a nondisclosure agreement regarding her relationship with the Blackwell family. Once the senator's candidacy for United States Senate became known, people would come crawling out of the woodwork, telling stories about future United States Senator James Blackwell.

If Janie went to the press, it could ruin everything Senator Blackwell had worked for.

As an aide to the senator's campaign, Alexander had to make sure that didn't happen.

If he succeeded, the senator promised him a spot in his office in Washington, DC, when he was elected.

When Alexander first realized Janie's mother's funeral was going on, he'd figured he'd cool his heels in the local café with a cup of coffee until he could check in to his cabin at the Double R Ranch and come up with a plan for meeting Janie and getting to know her.

It seemed almost too good to be true that the person who came to talk to him while he was pulled over, looking at his phone to find a place to go, was the very person he'd hoped to find.

Part of him felt like a total jerk, approaching her at her mother's funeral. But Janie had come to him. Had insisted he stay. Besides, Janie wasn't an innocent pastor's daughter. She'd been blackmailing the senator for years over the fact that his son, Bucky, had gotten her pregnant in college. The senator had been sending her money, justifying it as child support. But her financial demands had gotten worse lately, and she was threatening to go to the press with her lies.

What would she do if she knew about the senator's higher ambitions?

The only way to stop her was to give her a

final payoff and get her to sign a nondisclosure agreement. The senator had sent an investigator to do it, but Janie had thrown him out. It was up to Alexander to befriend her, earn her trust and figure out another way to get the job done.

And Alexander had the perfect story that would allow him to get close to her.

Only it wasn't a story. It was the truth.

That was one of the reasons Alexander had been chosen for this task. His mother was fascinated with tracing the family heritage for both herself and his father. For her birthday, he and his brother, William, bought everyone a DNA test kit, thinking what a great gift it would be to trace more of their family tree—well, some gift. Alexander and William had found out that their mother had been lying to them all for years about who their father was.

Their father, William Bennett, Senior, wasn't their father. No, that honor belonged to some rodeo cowboy their mom had met while she and their dad were fighting, and apparently, they had a one-night stand, leaving their mother pregnant. Alexander still couldn't wrap his head around the whole thing.

The cowboy, Cinco, died long ago in a bull-riding accident, but his father, Ricky Ruiz, was still alive and wanted to get to know Alexander and his brother. Something about righting the wrongs of the past, or some such nonsense.

While he figured out how to get to know Janie so he could have her sign the necessary paperwork, he would be here under the guise of meeting his long-lost family.

His mother hadn't given a second thought to the man she'd spent a night with. That's all that came to mind when he thought of the man who was supposedly their father. Their father had raised them, cared for them, been there through everything.

Bucky had never been involved with Janie's kid. It wasn't reasonable to expect him to keep forking over cash for a kid he didn't want. Child support, yes, but extortion, no. Which was why whatever agreement he got Janie to sign would include a final, but reasonable, payment.

Alexander and William didn't need money. They had a family who loved them. They didn't need a relationship with some long-lost grandfather. But it provided an excellent cover for Alexander's presence.

After parking his car where Janie indicated, Alexander couldn't help noticing she drove an older model that looked worse for the wear. With the kind of money the senator had been giving Janie, Alexander would think she'd drive a better car.

None of his business. It didn't matter to him one way or the other how Janie spent her ill-gotten gains. His only concern was getting her to sign the nondisclosure agreement and agree to a final payoff.

As he walked to the small garden area where he'd first seen Janie sitting when he arrived, he saw her exit the church, carrying two cups of coffee, balancing a plate on top of them.

He turned back toward her, striding in her direction. "Let me help you with that," he said.

Her soft smile erased some of the lines in her forehead, and despite the fragility in her expression, she looked…almost…pretty.

Okay, fine. Janie was gorgeous. Which seemed wrong to think at her mother's funeral, but Bucky had always dated knockouts. Janie looked a little like Bucky's fiancée, Corinne. The same wheat-blond hair and hazel eyes, though Corinne was a lot more put together.

Even though he'd seen dozens of pictures of her, there was an innocence to the woman standing before him he hadn't expected. Her hair was styled, not pulled back in a messy ponytail, and she looked much more neatly put together than the pictures he'd seen of her. True, he wasn't expecting her to resemble the drunk girl from college photos, but even the investigator's recent pictures made her out to look like a mess.

But, he supposed, she'd look her best for her mother's funeral.

"Thank you," she said as he took the plate off the top of the cups she carried. It was piled high with an assortment of cookies, pastries and a couple of bite-sized quiches.

"You didn't need to do all this for me," he said.

"I told you there was plenty of food. I would have grabbed some sandwiches too, but—" A dark expression crossed her face, then she shook her head. "This was the easiest for me to bring outside. Like I said, you're more than welcome to join us if you'd like to select some other things."

The investigator hadn't said she was so nice. His report hadn't given him much insight into the kind of person Janie was. The senator and Bucky had painted her as a flighty, greedy girl who only cared about material things.

But he couldn't see those qualities in the woman who took the time to think of a stranger's comfort at her mother's funeral.

"This is more than enough," he said as they

entered the garden area. It had a small table in the corner, and Janie walked in that direction.

In the summer, it was probably a beautiful space. But now, it felt bleak and cold.

"What brought you out here earlier?" he asked. "Were you close to the woman who died?"

He already knew the answer, but she didn't know that. He needed her to open up to him, to trust him, so she would be willing to talk to him about her son's father.

Janie looked down at the ground and didn't answer at first, but then said quietly, "She was my mother. I know it sounds terrible that I'm not in there, but I feel closer to her here. And I can't hear about everyone else's sadness when my own is so overwhelming."

The palpable grief in her words twisted Alexander's heart. He shouldn't be doing this now. But if not now, when? It wasn't like Janie had considered the convenience to the senator when she made her demands.

"I'm so sorry for your loss," Alexander said. "I'm sure a lot of people have said that to you already, but I don't know what else to say. I don't want to intrude."

She set her cup of coffee on the table and looked at him. "You're not. Please stop apologizing. I invited you. Right now, the one thing that would make me feel better about losing my mother is honoring her memory by helping someone else. Now tell me, what has you driving to a church and seeking the help of a pastor in the middle of the week?"

If that wasn't the best get-out-of-jail-free card he'd gotten in a long time, he didn't know what was.

Alexander took a deep breath. He'd been rehearsing his speech the entire way here, but now, he could barely remember the words.

"I just found out that the man I grew up thinking was my father isn't, and my biological father is the son of a man named Ricky Ruiz. My biological father is dead, but Ricky is still around. Ricky has been reaching out to me, and while part of me is curious, the other part is struggling with the idea of the whole thing. I thought the pastor at the local church where Ricky lived might have some insight."

He might be here for what Janie would perceive as less than honorable intentions, but at least in this, he told her the truth. He did want to know what it would be like to be at a family gathering of people who had brown hair and brown eyes and brown skin as opposed to blond hair, blue eyes and light skin. To look around the room and see people who resembled him.

But then he felt sick to his stomach at the thought of how admitting that felt like a betrayal to the family he knew and loved.

Then again, what was one more betrayal? Even though it felt wrong, gaining her trust when she seemed like such a nice lady, he had to remind himself that she was blackmailing the senator. It might feel like an ethical betrayal to hide his real intent in coming here, but he had to remind himself that he was doing this for the greater good.

This was about more than just getting the senator elected. For as long as Alexander could remember, he'd dreamed of becoming president of the United States and using that power to make the world a better place. Alexander knew he could make a difference in this world. And if he had to overcome some inconvenient circumstances in his family to make it happen, then he'd do so.

But the tender expression on Janie's face made Alexander wonder if this was going to be as easy a task as he'd originally thought.

Chapter Two

Ricky's grandson?

Janie stared at the man, and as she examined his features, she realized how much he resembled the large portrait of Cinco Ricky kept in the main house. Lighter skin, a little more serious and a sense of deep sadness in his eyes.

When she'd first spotted him, she'd been strangely drawn to him, and not just because she didn't recognize him as someone who belonged there. Funny how, when she was a teenager, she and her friends used to giggle about how cute they'd thought Cinco was.

Who would have ever thought she'd meet Cinco's son?

Her mom always told her that the best way to forget your own problems was to help someone else with theirs. Not that you should avoid your problems, but when the problem was something you couldn't do anything about, you might as well help someone else.

Maybe helping Ricky's grandson would take her mind off her grief, off the other problems in her life she needed to solve, and maybe things wouldn't seem so hard for her anymore.

"Our family is close to Ricky. I know a lot about his search for Cinco's children."

Ricky had been searching for his long-lost grandchild. So far, his investigation hadn't turned up the child he'd been looking for. Just Rachel, Janie's friend, and a pair of twins who'd refused contact with Ricky—but none of them were the child of Luanne, Cinco's wife.

So who was this man? One of the twins? Or Luanne's child?

Regardless, it had to be difficult, facing a family he hadn't known existed.

"It's very brave of you to come," she said. "I understand your hesitation, but let me reassure you that Ricky is truly one of the best people I know."

He only looked slightly relieved. "You shouldn't be troubling yourself with my problems. Your guests should be the focus of your attention. It's fine. I booked a cabin at the

Double R Ranch under a colleague's name, in case someone recognized mine. But I'm not sure I can go there. It's all too weird to me."

She couldn't imagine what he must be going through. There weren't any hotels nearby, just guest cabins for rent at Ricky's ranch. "Ricky will respect your privacy. If you need time to yourself, just tell him. He'll understand. He was wonderful when his granddaughter, Rachel, came to town."

If only she could read his expression. But whichever twin this was, he wasn't giving anything away.

"He didn't know about Rachel, either?"

Janie shook her head. "No. He and his son were estranged when his son died, leaving behind a pregnant wife. Ricky tried to locate her, but she didn't want to be found. He figured he'd committed an unpardonable sin in driving his son away, so he didn't start searching for her until recently. As he neared the end of his life, he wanted to make amends. He regretted driving his son away, and he wanted to have a relationship with his grandchild if he could. Well, turns out Cinco sowed a lot of wild oats. There are more grandchildren than he thought."

He closed his eyes like he was trying to process this information.

"Which one of Ricky's grandchildren are you?" Janie asked.

Opening his eyes, he looked at Janie. "Alexander. Alexander Bennett, and my twin brother is William, after our..." A look close to despair crossed Alexander's face. "How could she name him after our father, knowing he wasn't really?" His shoulders shook with a long sigh. "But he is our father, in every meaning of the word, except for what the DNA test says."

Even though she barely knew him, Janie found herself touching his arm gently. "That must be very difficult for you."

Alexander shrugged her off. "Difficult? You don't know the meaning of the word." He stared down at her, then shook his head slowly. "I'm sorry. Of course you know what it means. You're mourning the loss of your mother, and I'm being insensitive. You would probably say that at least I have a mother, right?"

The raw honesty and deep grief in his voice put an ache in Janie's heart. They were both going through hard things, and maybe that was why God had brought them together.

"It doesn't make what you're going through any less painful or any less important to talk about. You have just as much right to share your feelings as I do, so please don't feel guilty. Maybe it sounds silly, but talking to you is the first time I've felt some of my grief fall off me. How is this affecting the rest of your family?"

The desolate look he gave her made her almost wish she hadn't asked. Then he said, "It's tearing my whole family apart. You can't imagine what we're going through. I thought I could do this, but now I'm not so sure."

Janie scooted her chair closer to his. "You're right that I don't know anything about what you're going through. I probably appear to be on the enemy's side, but I'm willing to be your friend if you let me."

What she really wanted to do was take this man into her arms and hold him and tell him it was going to be all right. The expression on his face was just like Sam's when he was hurting. It was odd because she'd talked to hundreds of people in her lifetime, comforting them during a bad time, but something about Alexander uniquely twisted her heart. She didn't know why, but something deep inside her said that he needed her. That there was something different about him. Something special.

"There's a lot you don't understand," he said. "I know you're trying to be nice, and I appreciate that. But there's so much you don't know, and I don't think you're the right person for me to discuss this with."

Some men had a hard time talking to women, and her father said that sometimes, it was better for people of the same gender to counsel one another.

"Why don't I get my dad to come talk to you? After all, you did intend to speak to a pastor when you came here. Maybe he can give you the clarity you need."

Alexander shook his head. "He's burying his wife today. I can't intrude on him like this. I can't intrude on you like this."

Ugh. Why did he have to keep harping on being an intrusion?

Like Janie, her father had been keeping busy since her mother's death.

How was she supposed to get Alexander, and everyone else for that matter, to understand that helping others was the only way they were going to get through her mother's death?

The back church doors opened, and people began filtering out. She recognized Ricky in the crowd.

"Ricky's right over there," she said. "I know you said you weren't sure if you're ready, but maybe it would be better if you just pulled the Band-Aid off? My son, Sam, cries and cries when I tell him I'm going to take his Band-Aids off. But I've found it causes way less trauma if I just rip it off when he's not expecting it. I think that's true for a lot of things in life."

Alexander nodded thoughtfully. "I suppose that's one way to handle it. If it doesn't work out, I could always get in my car and drive home."

There were more positive answers, but at least it wasn't a no. "Wait right here," she said. She jumped up and made her way to Ricky as fast as she could without it looking like there was a fire. When she got to Ricky, he was talking good-naturedly with some of their rancher friends.

"Excuse me, Ricky. I was hoping we could have a quick private word with you."

It definitely wasn't the smoothest thing she'd ever done, but since he'd given her mother's eulogy and everyone thought she was in the depths of grief, they all smiled cordially, stepping away so Janie could take him by the arm and lead him in the direction of the garden.

"I have some interesting news for you," she said when they were out of earshot of the others. "Remember those twins of Cinco's who wanted nothing to do with you?"

As Ricky nodded, she continued. "One of

them, Alexander, is in the garden. He came here first to gather his courage to meet you, only he came at a bad time. And now he's not sure what to do."

Ricky nodded somberly. "I wasn't ever expecting to meet either of them. They made it very clear they wanted nothing to do with me. But clearly the Lord is working in his heart, so I'll do my best to be gentle with him."

Janie smiled at him. "I can't imagine you being hard on him."

As they reentered the garden, Alexander's back was to them, like he was still considering running.

"Alexander. Ricky is here," Janie said.

Alexander turned around, and he still wore the same lost little boy expression he'd had when she'd first begun speaking with him.

Ricky introduced himself. "I'm your biological grandfather. I know that must sound very strange to you. You don't have to call me Grandpa or Gramps or anything like that. You can just call me Ricky. If you'd like, no one but Janie and me have to know who you are. Though I'm sure Rachel would love to meet you."

Alexander took a step forward. "Thanks. I appreciate that. I'm still trying to wrap my head around all this. You have to understand, my dad's great." He shook his head. "The best father any man could ever ask for. Bill Bennett, that's him, is the most standup guy you'd ever want to meet. He raised us right. He took us to Little League, went to our school activities, was there to lend an ear whenever we needed him. I was just out fishing with him last weekend. So to find out that he is—"

"He's still your father," Ricky said. "I respect that. It's good that you honor him. It sounds like you had a great life growing up, and I don't want to take any of that from you. I'm trying to do the right thing, and I don't rightly know what that is. But we're family, and I'm here for you if you want me to be. Anything that happens is your choice."

What was supposed to be an easy job was now turning into a nightmare. One of epic proportions. The kind where you felt like you were falling with no bottom in sight.

All he needed to do was to get Janie to sign some papers. They were sitting in his briefcase in the back seat of his car. He simply had to walk over, grab the papers and tell Janie to sign them.

Of course, the private investigator had already tried that. And she'd promptly thrown him out. It would've been nice if his investigator had told him that today was her mother's funeral, but he supposed he should have done that legwork on his own.

And now, having spoken with Janie, having seen the selfless way she'd tried to comfort him when he should be trying to comfort her over her mother's death, he couldn't imagine her as the Jezebel she'd been painted as. But he'd seen the checks, the notes, demanding more money.

He'd heard that con artists were able to con people because of how kind and sweet they appeared at first.

And then there was the other problem.

The man standing before him. Ricky. His grandfather. Except Ricky was also being completely understanding and kind.

This whole thing just got a lot more complicated.

Even though he knew he'd be dealing with difficult emotions, he hadn't been prepared for just how difficult it would be. Part of him still wanted to run. But he had to figure out how to put his emotions aside so he could get his job done.

Alexander took a step forward. "I appreciate that. I'll be honest, William is upset with me for coming. But at least it takes off some of the heat of him being mad at our mom for cheating on our dad. I'm kind of mad at her, too, but if she didn't do what she did, we wouldn't be here. And I don't know what to make of that."

Janie gave him that gentle smile he'd come to expect. Why did she have to be the opposite of what he'd been expecting?

"In the Bible, there is a story about Joseph. His brothers sold him into slavery. I don't know if you know the story, but Joseph went through a lot of difficult times because of his brothers' actions. However, Joseph rose to prominence and was able to help everyone, including his brothers, because of it. In the end, the brothers apologized for what they did to him, but Joseph tells them that while they intended to harm him, God used it for good. We all do wrong things, but God can still bring good out of them. Infidelity is a terrible thing, but look at the blessing it brought your family—two men they love."

Alexander shrugged, trying not to let her words get to him. Yes, she'd essentially said that his struggles had been used by God in a good way. If God was as good as they all said He was, why would he need something bad to make something good? Wouldn't the good thing have happened anyway?

"I probably heard it," Alexander said. "Our family isn't much into church. I mean, we go at Christmas and Easter and stuff, but I can't say that I ever studied the Bible."

He felt ashamed at admitting that in a churchyard. But he supposed if he hadn't been struck down by lightning for being here without pure intentions, God wasn't going to smite him for admitting that now.

"It's okay," Janie said. "I know people who aren't as familiar with the Bible can't relate to everything I say. But I've got a spare Bible you can have to read yourself if you'd like."

Right. He'd forgotten he was talking to a preacher's daughter. Funny, since he had a whole file on all of Janie's sins. Was that how she justified those bad actions? Thinking God would somehow use it for good?

Alexander shook his head. Not his problem.

But what was his problem was that in spite of his mistrust of her, he couldn't help liking her. She was truly one of the nicest people he'd met. *Nice* wasn't even the word for it. Janie seemed too kind and generous to be blackmailing the senator.

Honestly, if he wasn't secretly trying to get her to sign a nondisclosure agreement, and they weren't at her mother's funeral, he'd want to ask her out for coffee or something. Funny, since Alexander didn't do relationships. At some point, he would need to find a good wife to stand by him and be his partner in his political aspirations. The trouble was, every woman he met was either too full of ambitions herself, or lacked the kind of impeccable record the future president of the United States would need. That was how so many politicians fell from grace. One little skeleton in the closet, and it was all over.

A skeleton like Janie's, blackmailing an upstanding family over her illegitimate child? Forget about it. The press would have a field day with her, and it would ruin everything he had worked for.

As it was, Janie's blackmailing ways just might ruin the aspirations of a fine man like Senator James Blackwell.

He had to shut any thoughts of Janie being a nice girl out of his mind. He already knew she was bad news.

Which left the man standing before him. Ricky. He also seemed like a nice guy, and the more he learned about him during this brief conversation, the more he wondered if perhaps he had been too hasty in immediately dismissing him.

He didn't know what he was afraid of. William was already so mad at him for ignoring his calls, and his father had gruffly told him that he had to do what he had to do. Which probably meant that his father didn't like it, but wasn't going to stop him. Kind of like when he'd gone out of state for college. His mother was still so busy begging for forgiveness that regardless of what he did, she wasn't going to argue or complain.

What did Alexander have to lose in giving Ricky a chance?

"I guess it wouldn't hurt to get to know you," Alexander said. "I had one of my assistants book a cabin for me at the ranch under his name, so I'll be staying there for a while."

He left out the part about getting Janie to sign the agreement. That needed to be his focus when he talked to Janie. Not thinking how nice she was, but how she was hurting the senator. If she wanted to remind him of the Bible, he'd just remind himself that he was pretty sure the Bible said somewhere that wolves often appeared in sheep's clothing. Janie might look like a sheep, but she was really a wolf.

"Thank you," Ricky said. "That means the world to me. I'm headed there now, so you could follow me if you like."

The encouraging smile Janie gave him made him feel slightly queasy. Maybe he needed to go back and look at the drunk Janie pictures and reread her blackmail notes to remind him of her true character.

The last note had been two months ago. Her mom had been sick then—maybe she had needed treatments and couldn't afford them. Which sort of meant that Janie was justified in her actions. But she couldn't keep treating the senator like her personal ATM.

"That would be good," Alexander said. "I don't feel right hanging around a funeral for someone I don't know."

Janie gave him another encouraging smile. "It's all right," she said. "Like I told you, both my father and I would be happy to counsel you or pray with you. Ministry is what my family does. The best way we could honor my mother's memory is to continue helping those in need. It's what she would want."

He should take her up on her offer. After all, that was his real purpose in being here. To get close enough to her to get her to trust him enough to talk about the senator, then to convince her to sign the agreement.

But the conflicting emotions he felt in being with her was going to make it hard.

"I agree," Ricky said. "I meant what I said when I told you I want what's best for you."

What was best for him was for his mom not to be a liar, cheater... Alexander shook his head, trying to remember how much his mom loved him. Of all the ways she'd been there for him, and had been an excellent mother. Until this revelation, he'd have said that she was the perfect mother.

He was doing his best to accept this change, but he still wasn't sure how to accept a new family.

Before he could figure out an answer to give Ricky, Janie waved at someone behind him.

Alexander turned to see a woman who looked remarkably like a female version of himself, holding hands with a little boy and a little girl.

"Rachel! Over here!"

Janie stepped next to Alexander and said quietly, "I'm sorry. She was watching my son, and I know she needs to get home. I won't tell her who you are until you're ready."

When the little boy caught sight of Janie, he let go of Rachel's hand and came running toward her. "Mom!"

Rachel and the little girl followed, and Alexander couldn't help staring. It had been one thing to see a man with brown skin call himself his grandfather. But this woman… he didn't need a DNA test to know she was his sister.

A sister.

When he was little, he'd tried to trade William in for a sister. His mom used to tell a story of how he'd approached a woman in the park who had a bunch of little girls and asked her if she wanted to trade. The woman had laughed him off, and when Alexander was older, his mom had admitted that they'd had trouble conceiving more children.

Another reason he wondered about the whole blessing-in-disguise aspect of his mother's infidelity. Maybe his father couldn't have children, so this had given them the children they wouldn't have otherwise had.

"Sorry we took so long," Rachel said. "The kids were having fun on the playground, and I hated to tear them away."

Janie stood and smiled at her friend. "It's okay. I felt like I owed you an apology for taking so long. This man needed some prayer, and I hated to leave him."

The smile in Rachel's eyes did a funny thing in Alexander's heart. It was like he'd known her forever, even though they'd never spoken. This was the sister he'd always wanted. He wanted to tell her how he and William used to dress up their dog in girl clothes to pretend she was their sister. How, even though he'd never admitted it to anyone else, he used to talk to an imaginary sister when he was annoyed with William.

They said twins were supposed to have a special bond, but it didn't replace the longing in Alexander to have a little sister to spoil.

Based on what he'd learned from the DNA information, he and William were older than Rachel by about six months. She was their little sister.

"I hope we aren't intruding," Rachel said. "We could go back to the playground for a while if you need us to."

Great. Another nice woman. Life was so much easier when he'd been painting them all as enemies in his mind.

"Not at all," Janie said. "He's a guest at the ranch, and he was thinking of following Ricky back there so he can get settled."

Her words made it easy to decide what to do. He would follow Ricky to the ranch, get checked in to his cabin, review Janie's file and make contact again.

"Oh, good," Rachel said. "We're headed there as well. Wanda wanted me to let you know that you're welcome at the house if you want to get away for a while. She's not inviting other guests, just you and your dad, if you're looking for a little peace and quiet."

The relief on Janie's face was evident, and

once again, Alexander felt bad for making Janie's mother's funeral about him.

"Can we? Please?" Sam asked, looking so earnest and cute.

Alexander had seen photos of the little boy, and even though there were questions of his paternity when Janie had initially gotten pregnant, there was no denying this little boy was Bucky's. Funny how genetics never lied.

He understood that Bucky hadn't been ready to be a father when Janie had gotten pregnant, but seeing this cute kid in front of him made Alexander wonder why Bucky hadn't stepped up anyway. For all of Janie's faults, she'd done a great job on her own. The senator had said that Janie hadn't wanted Bucky to be a father, she just wanted a paycheck. Regardless, if it had been Alexander, he'd have wanted to be in this little boy's life.

"Mom!" Sam said, tugging at her hand. "Please?"

Janie looked over at Ricky, who shrugged. "Wanda is the real boss at the ranch."

Then he turned to Alexander. "Wanda is my housekeeper. She runs a tight ship, but I wouldn't have it any other way. You're welcome to join us if you like, or you can get settled in your cabin. Whatever you want."

Ricky's speech made Rachel look more intently at Alexander. "You look familiar. Do I know you?"

It was now or never. He could tell her that this was the first time they'd met, which was technically the truth. But he'd already told so many half-truths, it was weighing on his conscience. If he wanted a relationship with his sister, the only place to start was here.

When he opened his mouth to speak, his throat was tight, like it was clogged.

"I'm your half brother, Alexander Bennett."

The words came out awkwardly, but they were out. Judging by the look on her face, she knew who he was.

"Oh," she said. "I see."

"I know I came at a bad time. I didn't realize—"

Janie touched his arm. "I told you, it's okay. You didn't know. I promise, this is what my mom would have wanted. She prayed so earnestly for Ricky to reunite with his grandchildren, and it seems kind of perfect that you'd show up at her funeral."

"I didn't think about that," Ricky said, rubbing his chin. "The last thing your mother prayed for for me when she was able to speak was to have my family restored. I'm sure she and my Rosie are rejoicing in heaven today to see it."

His voice caught, and the emotion in his

eyes was almost too much for Alexander to bear. He wasn't an answered prayer. He was going to be the end of the gravy train Janie had been counting on. Sure, there'd be a financial settlement. But after that, the greedy woman would be on her own.

Would his newfound family be so welcoming to him then?

Before Alexander could think of a response, a cowboy approached. "Ricky, a fire's been reported off Old Bridge Road near the campground. The volunteer fire department is on its way, but since it borders our far pasture, we should send a crew as well."

Alexander followed Ricky's gaze in what must be the direction of Old Bridge Road. A plume of smoke snaked into the sky, thick and menacing. Others must have received the same phone call, because several men were running to their trucks. Rachel and Janie looked at each other, then pulled their children close.

"Thanks, Hunter," Ricky said. "Send a crew to help the fire department, and then get another set of men to work on creating a fire break to keep it from spreading to the pasture. I don't want to lose our winter grazing."

Hunter nodded. "Good plan. I'll get right on it."

As Hunter turned to leave, his cell phone rang. From the conversation on his end, it sounded like people were being evacuated.

Alexander looked at Rachel and Janie, who seemed to be trying to decipher what was being said on the other end of the phone. Whatever concern Rachel had about his identity was now replaced by the greater concern over the fire.

"How bad is it?" Ricky asked when Hunter ended the call.

"Spreading fast," Hunter said. "They're evacuating everyone west of the old highway. The fire department is going to need all the help they can get. The forest service is sending people, but they're at least an hour away."

Ricky looked thoughtful, but before he could answer, another man joined them and they stepped out of earshot. Alexander didn't intend to eavesdrop, but even without hearing the references to fire, the way the men pointed at the smoke with concern on their faces, he knew the situation was rapidly growing worse.

"We should do something to help," Janie said to Rachel.

Rachel shook her head. "You go relax. It's your mother's funeral."

"I can't relax. Not when the town is in danger. Old Bridge Road isn't too far from here. Besides, I feel better being useful. Why don't you take the kids to the ranch, and I'll join you when I can?"

For a moment, Rachel looked like she was going to argue, but then she nodded. "All right. They'll be in the way here. But you know, at some point, you're going to have to slow down, and when you do, you're going to have to deal with your grief."

Then Rachel held her hands out to the kids. "Okay, guys, let's head out to the ranch."

The kids ignored her outstretched hands and raced off. She shrugged, then turned to Alexander. "It was nice meeting you, I guess. I don't know if you're sticking around or not, but—"

She looked like she had something else to say, but then she shrugged again. Alexander supposed he didn't blame her for the lackluster greeting and welcome. Earlier in the year, when he'd first found out about his relationship to Ricky, one of Ricky's representatives had contacted him, asking if he or his brother would be willing to donate a kidney to Rachel. They'd refused, and while he'd heard that Rachel had gotten a kidney from another source, he felt guilty for his refusal. Especially now that he'd met her.

"Sam," Janie called. "Where's my hug?"

The little boy turned around and ran back to her. Janie wrapped him in her arms and hugged him tight before releasing him. The bond between mother and son was apparent, and for all of Janie's other faults, she clearly loved her child deeply.

Sam ran back to his friend just as Ricky and the other two men finished their discussion. Ricky turned his attention back to Alexander and Janie.

"The fire is heading toward the Peterson ranch. But there's no one to evacuate their animals since they're on vacation. Janie, I know you house-sat for them in the past. Tom Riley has been doing it this time, but he's on his way to deal with the fire. Can you go by the Peterson ranch and get their animals to safety? That old dog of Jack's will bite anyone he doesn't know. Do you think you can get him to come to you?"

Janie nodded. "Of course. Dobby and I are great friends. But what about his horses? Do you have someone who can get them?"

Ricky's brow furrowed. "I was hoping you would get them when you got the dog."

Janie shook her head. "I don't know how to drive a truck and trailer. I've only done it once, and I ended up in a ditch. Do you have anyone else?"

With the way everyone seemed to be rushing about, and the expression on Ricky's face, Alexander was pretty sure the answer would be no. While he had come here with a specific objective in mind, there was a more pressing issue at hand. He didn't know anything about fighting fires, but there was one way he could help.

Alexander turned to Ricky. "What kind of truck and trailer are we talking about? I've never driven a horse trailer before, but my family often goes boating, and I've pulled the boat countless times. It can't be too much different, can it?"

The relief on the older man's face was evident as he nodded. "It's the same. You've probably never handled horses, though, have you?"

Alexander shrugged. "I haven't." Then he turned to Janie. "But I'm assuming if you're going to get the dog, you also know how to get the horses, right?"

Her small smile warmed his heart. He wasn't supposed to want to make her smile. Ultimately, he was going to hurt her, and he didn't know how to make that easier. But maybe, working together for the common good, he could find a way to soften the blow and show Janie that it was to her advantage to sign the paperwork.

Except, even as he told himself that, it felt like a lie.

Which was ridiculous, because Alexander knew this was the best solution for everyone.

If only Janie didn't look at him like he was a hero as she said, "I can take care of the animals if you can drive."

"Then what are we all standing here yammering about?" Ricky said. "I'm going to ride with Ty back to the ranch. You take my truck. You can load the horses into the Petersons' trailer. Marcus said it was parked in its usual spot when he came to town this morning."

"Great," Alexander said. "Let me just get my briefcase and wallet out of my car."

Once Alexander had what he needed, Janie guided him in the direction of Ricky's truck. It was a good thing he was parked on the street, and not in the parking lot, where people were so frantically trying to get out. It was a nice truck, so no wonder Janie had been apprehensive about taking it.

"We're headed that way," Janie said, pointing at the thick plume of smoke in the distance as Alexander slid onto the leather seat.

He'd been taught to run away from fire, and now he was running into it. While it felt somewhat strange to him, he couldn't help thinking that was also what he was doing by being here in the first place. Running straight into the fire with his mixed-up emotions.

"It seems strange to have a wildfire in November," Alexander said, trying to take his mind off those emotions.

"It's been a dry year," she said. "While we don't usually get much snow in the fall, we haven't had any, so add in the dry summer, and everything is a tinderbox. You must have noticed all the signs about the fire danger on your way here."

He'd spent his whole life traveling through Colorado, seeing signs about what level the fire danger was, but until now, he hadn't realized just how important they were.

"I guess you never think it's going to happen to you," he said.

Which pretty well summed up the events leading to this day, this moment. He'd never imagined his father would be some dead rodeo cowboy, or that the monster woman he was chasing was actually a tenderhearted person who cared for others, or that he'd be willingly putting himself in danger.

But what other choice did he have?

Chapter Three

Janie shouldn't have been surprised at how eager Alexander had been to help. After all, helping others was a large part of who Ricky was. Alexander might not have been raised in that family, but some genes ran strong.

The closer they got to the fire, the more desperate the situation looked. The smoke was so thick, it was hard to see in front of them. Even though the truck windows were closed, Janie could still smell the unmistakable scent of fire.

She stole a glance at Alexander, who appeared intensely focused on the road. Was it wrong to think about how good-looking he was? Seeing the compassion in his eyes as he'd offered to help made him even more attractive to her. Crazy, since she hadn't thought about dating in years. Not when she had a son to raise. She couldn't remember the last time she'd found a man attractive because she'd worked so hard to shut that emotion down.

Alexander glanced back at her. "Your little boy is really cute. You and your husband must be very proud. I'm sorry I didn't get a chance to meet him."

Not this again. Everyone always made the same assumption about her and Sam, especially since she was a pastor's daughter.

Bracing herself for the coming judgment, Janie said, "I don't have a husband. I'm not married. Never have been. I don't talk about Sam's father. He's not in our lives. He has never been, and never will be. I made a mistake when I was younger, and I've repented. But God chose to give me the greatest blessing of my life in spite of it."

Someday it wouldn't feel so terrible giving that answer. But the silence between them was deafening.

"I'm sorry, I didn't mean to pry," Alexander said. "I was just making conversation. I was pretty sure you didn't want to talk about your mother, and I didn't know what else to say. I didn't mean to offend you. He seems like a good kid, though."

Now it was her turn to feel bad. Alexander had just been trying to be considerate of her grief. Her mother used to tell her that she had too big of a chip on her shoulder over being a single mother, and seeing the way Alexander responded to her explanation, she had to wonder if perhaps her mother was right after all.

Even in avoiding her grief, she was still coming face to face with the pain of her loss.

"I'm sorry," she said. "I get a little defensive about the subject. It's just frustrating that everyone assumes that as the pastor's daughter, I'm perfect. But I make mistakes just like everyone else. In this case, my sin is very evident, so I'm a little self-conscious about it."

"It's okay," Alexander said. "I can't imagine how difficult your situation must be. Raising a child on your own, one parent, one income—it can't be easy. And then to feel like people are judging you, I'm sure, is even worse. I just don't understand how a man can father a child, then choose not to be involved in that child's life."

It was sweet to see how readily he came to her defense. Funny how all the men in her life seemed to do that, but not the man she'd needed. She'd given up any thoughts of Sam's father being involved in his life. Especially after that creepy investigator's visit. But it didn't mean that as she'd seen her friends find the love and wholeness in a new family, she didn't sometimes long for that for herself.

Though Ricky had been concerned about roadblocks on the way to the Peterson ranch, they didn't encounter any. But when they arrived, the smoke was thick, and the horses in the paddock were antsy, squealing like they knew something bad was happening.

Alexander put the truck in Park. "I'm assuming that trailer by the barn is the one we're supposed to use," he said.

"Yes. I'll get the dog first, and if you can pull the trailer close to that gate, it'll be easier for me to load the horses."

She pointed at where she wanted him to go, but she almost didn't need to. The horses were already lined up there, like they knew it was their only means of escape.

Then he looked around the truck, like he was searching for something. He reached into the center console, then pulled out a couple of bandanas.

"Take this. Cover your nose and mouth with it. I'm not sure how much good it will do, but we shouldn't be breathing in all this stuff."

She took the bandana. "How do you know this?"

Alexander shrugged. "I've seen a few movies with fires. Everyone has protective stuff over their nose and mouth. I know this isn't specialized equipment, but it's got to be better than nothing."

He had a point. One more reason to be grateful he'd come with her. And even though his questions had made her think about uncomfortable topics, he was good company.

Was it weird to like a man she'd barely met?

"Hurry," Alexander said. "I think the fire is moving faster than they told us."

He didn't need to tell her twice. She jumped out of the truck and raced toward the house. Thankfully, it was unlocked, which was typical in their small town. City people often thought they were crazy, but most of them never had any reason to lock their doors. Ricky did, of course, at his ranch, but that was because it was a guest ranch, and guests expected a certain level of privacy.

As she entered the house, a text came through on the phone from Ricky, asking her to grab the small portable document safe out of the bedroom closet. The Petersons had asked for more items from their home, but the fire was spreading quickly, and there wouldn't be time to get anything else.

Dobby barked at her from his kennel in the laundry room, not just because she was an intruder, but also because he could probably smell the smoke rapidly filling the house. Even though the fire was still a ways away, the interior of the house was starting to feel warm. Too warm. She went to the bedroom first, and grabbed the safe. She paused at the dresser, where an old photo of Jack and Connie Peterson at their wedding stood proudly. Maybe there wasn't time to save everything, but they would probably be glad for this one sentimental item.

The safe was small and had a handle so she could carry it like a briefcase. She went to the dog's kennel and let him out, then put him on his leash.

"Come on, buddy, we've got to hurry."

Dobby barked like he agreed, and they rushed out to the truck, where Alexander was just finishing hooking up the trailer.

She put the dog in the back seat of the truck along with the items she'd grabbed from the house. On her way to the tack room, she said to Alexander, "When you're finished with that, can you go back into the house, in the laundry room, and grab Dobby's kennel?"

"I have one more thing to hook up, then I can do it. Is there anything I can do to help with the horses?"

Janie shook her head. "Not if you don't

know what you're doing. But thanks anyway. This shouldn't take long."

She grabbed halters and ropes for each of the four horses, grateful that Jack Peterson always kept his tack room organized. The first horse, Molly, was easy to catch, and she loaded her into the trailer without complications. The next two were also easy, but when she got to the fourth, a stubborn mare named Lady, she wouldn't let Janie get the halter on.

"Come on, Lady, we've got to get you out of here."

Lady reared, nearly knocking Janie to the ground. Alexander ran to her.

"Are you all right?"

Janie nodded. "Stand back. Lady is spooked as it is, and I don't want you getting hurt. You've still got to drive us out of here."

Though Alexander took a step back, she could see that he was watching closely.

"Do horses like treats or something?" he asked. "Could we calm her down and move her into the trailer with one? I could see if they have apples or carrots in the house. I've seen people give them to horses on TV."

If they weren't in such a dire situation, she might have given him a hard time, but they didn't have time for that. "I left the door to the tack room open. I think I saw a bag of horse treats on the shelf. Grab it."

Though she didn't like rewarding bad behavior with treats, if it meant getting this horse to cooperate in a dangerous situation, Janie was willing to give it a try. In the distance, she could see flames cresting over one of the hills.

They didn't have much time. Lady had to load within the next couple of minutes, or they were going to have to set her loose and hope for the best—otherwise, they were all going to die.

Janie's phone rang. It was Ricky.

"You've got to get out of there now," Ricky said. "The wind has picked up. Even the firefighters are leaving the area because the fire is burning too hot and too fast."

"I can see it," Janie said. "Lady won't load. Alexander went to get some treats to see if we can coax her in, but I'm not sure if it's going to work."

"That dumb mare." Ricky made a disgusted noise. "I told Jack not to buy her, but Connie loves that stupid horse. See what you can do, but you've got to be out within the next five minutes."

Janie hung up and focused on the horse. Lady reared again.

Alexander arrived, holding the bag of treats.

"Come on, nice horse," he said. "I've got a yummy bag of treats for you. Besides, if you don't come with us, you're going to die."

It was kind of cute, the singsong voice he used, trying to cajole the horse into obedience. It was too bad horses didn't understand what people said. But for whatever reason, Lady did calm down.

Janie grabbed a treat out of the bag. "Come on, girl."

She held the treat out to Lady, but Lady snorted and backed away.

"Let me try," Alexander said.

This was a bad idea on so many levels, but Lady had calmed down at the sound of his voice.

"Put the treat in your hand and hold it flat, or else she's going to bite you."

Alexander did as she told him, and Lady took a step toward him.

"Good girl," Alexander said in his silly voice. "You're such a good girl. We're going to get you to safety."

Lady took the treat from his hand, and it gave Janie the chance to get the bridle on. Immediately, Lady pulled back, but Alexander started talking to her again.

"It's okay." He placed another treat on his hand. "Come on, girl, we're going to help you."

Lady took the treat, but when Janie tried getting the horse to move, she remained where she was. Alexander seemed to understand what was going on, so he took a few steps closer to the trailer and held out another treat to her.

"Come on. You know you want another treat."

He seemed to know the way to this mare's heart, because Lady did exactly what Alexander was trying to get her to do. She came toward him and took the treat. Then Alexander went to the trailer and did it again. Lady took the treat, but Janie couldn't get her to go into the trailer.

"This probably isn't a good idea," Alexander said, "but I'll get in the trailer with her."

He went into the trailer, then held out another treat. "Let's go, sweetie. We're almost there."

Alexander was right. It wasn't the smartest idea to get into a trailer with the horse who was already spooked. But he seemed to have Lady's number. Because she stepped right up into the trailer just as easily as the other three had.

Alexander scooted around the horse. "Okay, girl, don't kick me or bite me. We've got to get out of here."

He hopped out of the trailer, allowing Janie to secure the back, and they were quickly on their way. She had to give him credit—for someone with no horse experience, he'd done a good job.

As they pulled out of the driveway, Janie could see the fire lapping at the trees at the farthest edge of the pasture.

"You need to go as fast as you feel safe," Janie said. "The fire is almost here."

She said a prayer for their safety, and also for the Peterson family and the devastation they were going to feel at losing everything. Yes, she'd saved their precious animals, a safe and a wedding picture. But Ricky had said their list was longer, and she wished she'd had time to get it all.

Alexander didn't need to be told twice, and Janie was grateful for the fact that the Petersons lived off the paved road, not a dirt one like so many of the ranchers. That would have slowed them down considerably.

Janie's phone rang again. "Ricky, it's okay. We're on our way back to town. We got everything."

"You're going to have to find another way. The fire crossed County Road 42, so you're not going to be able to get through. Turn around and go south, then cut across to the east along the old canal."

"The fire is dangerously close to the Peterson ranch. I don't know if we'll make it past," Janie said. "Is there another route?"

Before Ricky could answer, the phone crackled and went dead. Janie stared down at it.

"What's wrong?" Alexander asked.

Janie dialed Ricky's number, but she was immediately greeted with an "all circuits are busy" message. She hung up and looked over at Alexander.

"I lost my connection to Ricky. He said the fire has compromised the main road we need to get back to town, but the route he wants us to take is right past the ranch, where the fire is. I don't know what to do."

Alexander slowed the truck, then pulled over to the side of the road. "Ricky has more information about the overall path of the fire than we do. But I don't know the area. You tell me what you think is best, and we'll do it."

As much as she hated to admit it, Alexander was right. Ricky did have more information about the best route to get back to town, even if it sounded crazy to her.

"We should probably go the way Ricky said, but I'm scared."

The admission was harder to make than she thought, but in the back of her mind, she could hear her mother telling her that she should never be afraid because God was with her wherever she went.

"Turn around and go back toward the Peterson ranch. Go as fast as you can, and about a mile past, you're going to turn left, but the turn isn't obvious, so I'll let you know when we're coming up on it. I know you said you aren't much of a churchgoer, but if you have any faith in God, you will pray with all your heart for His protection, and just in case, you might want to make right whatever you need to make right with Him."

Alexander took one hand off the wheel and reached for hers. "I have faith that we're going to make it through. And when we do, I'll let you talk to me about God."

The warmth of his hand as he squeezed hers gave her courage. Strength. And as she felt the whisper of her mother's prayers in her heart, she had the same faith that they were going to make it.

"You have a deal," she said. "Talking to people who aren't sure they believe in God is one of my favorite things to do."

As they headed back toward the Peterson

ranch, Janie could see the fire growing in the hills. Too close for comfort.

But when they got to the turnoff, it looked like there was logic in Ricky's recommendation to take this route. From the top of the small hill they were on, Janie could see the fire spreading in the distance. This old canal road would take them farthest from it.

Alexander must have come to the same conclusion she had because as he slowed to make the turn, allowing for the difference between driving on a paved road and a barely used dirt road, he let out a sigh of relief.

"We're finally headed away from the danger," he said.

Janie took a deep breath as she nodded slowly. "We are. It doesn't mean we can take our time, but at least we aren't racing against the fire for now."

In the back seat, Dobby barked, like he too was relieved they were finally headed for safety.

Janie reached behind her and petted him. "Good boy."

Then she turned back to Alexander. "You got his kennel? I didn't even ask when we were at the house, but I suppose it doesn't matter now."

"I did. It's in the bed of the pickup. I hope

it's okay, but it looked like Mrs. Peterson had been working on some old scrapbooks on the dining room table. The pictures were black-and-white, like they were heirlooms. So I grabbed those, too. It sounds kind of dumb, but I thought it might give her some comfort, knowing her whole house has burned down."

Janie smiled at him. "I did the same thing. I took the wedding picture they kept on the dresser. It isn't much, but I'm sure they'll be happy to have it."

There was something very tender and sweet about Alexander and his thoughtfulness through this whole process. He'd come, unsure of the welcome he'd receive, or if he even wanted to be here. And yet he jumped right in because their community needed his help.

"I know you didn't sign up for this when you came here," Janie said. "But I hope you know just how much we appreciate it."

No, he hadn't signed up for this. Alexander still wasn't sure what he'd been thinking, driving toward the fire, calming a crazy horse, then getting in a trailer with it when it could stomp him to death.

But what other choice did he have? He wouldn't have been able to walk away and feel good about himself, knowing these people needed his help. In some ways, it deepened his resolve to go into politics, because he liked knowing he was helping people. And with the power of political office, he could help more people.

The old canal road obviously wasn't driven very often. But since they were headed away from the fire, they could take things more slowly. Alexander felt his muscles relax as they got farther down the road.

"That has been the closest to death I've ever come," he said, trying to laugh and make a joke of it.

"You know, even though we did make a deal that I could talk to you about Jesus, I don't want you to feel obligated just because you had a near-death experience. You don't owe God your allegiance for saving you. God just wants you to love Him."

He could tell there was more to it than that, but Janie was trying to be gentle with him. She was giving him an out, which he appreciated. But the peace he felt in his heart told him that maybe it was time for him to know God. Not because, as Janie had suggested, they had just cheated death. But because he wanted to know more about whatever it was that had brought such a deep peace to his heart.

"It's okay," Alexander said. "I genuinely do want to hear more. But first, you should check your cell signal and see if we can get one now. Ricky is probably worried."

Plus, even though he did want to know more, he still needed to figure out the discrepancy between knowing he needed to get Janie to sign the papers and the fact that something about it felt wrong. Janie wasn't the woman she'd been depicted as. But he'd seen for himself all the evidence of her blackmail.

Surely she wasn't that good of a liar. But what other explanation was there?

"Ricky?"

The silence after Janie's question told him that she'd been able to get through. Then she said, "I think we're losing some of the cell towers. We made it to the old canal road, but it's slow going because the road is in such bad condition."

She listened to whatever he had to say, her face falling with every word.

When she hung up, she looked devastated.

"The winds have shifted, and the fire is headed toward town."

Alexander's stomach sank. How could

there have been so much devastation in such a short period?

"Is there any hope?"

"There's always hope," Janie said. "You should start seeing planes dropping retardant on the fire soon. And we're getting fire crews from elsewhere in the state. They're starting to arrive now. But it doesn't look good."

Alexander could see a crossroads in the distance.

"Turn right there," Janie said. "It'll take us around town the long way, and then we can cut across to Ricky's ranch."

The dejected tone of her voice made Alexander's heart hurt. What would it be like, having everything you loved threatened like this?

"Will your home be okay? I don't mind risking it if there are valuables you want to get."

Janie shook her head. "I don't know. But Ricky specifically said it was too dangerous for us to go to town. He told us to take the long way to be safe, but also to stay out of the way of people being evacuated and emergency responders trying to do their jobs. I have insurance if my house burns down. My most valued possession is already at Ricky's ranch. As long as I have Sam, I have everything."

Her words humbled him. All along, they'd been thinking that Janie's motivation was all about money. But what if it wasn't? What if there was something more to what Janie wanted?

However, if her house burned down, even with the insurance money, she would be desperate for funds. It would be so easy to get her to sign then.

But how could he take advantage of that level of desperation?

He might not yet have had that talk with Janie about God, but he prayed with all his heart that God would spare Janie's home and the homes of her loved ones—because he wasn't sure he could live with himself if that was how he'd get her to sign those papers.

Chapter Four

Everything was gone.

Janie sat on the twisted remains of her favorite bench in her mother's prayer garden at the church and surveyed the town. The entire northeast part of town was gone. Nothing more than charred remains.

The fire had ripped through their town four days ago, and emergency responders were just now letting people back in to survey the damage.

The sound of footfalls behind her made her turn.

"Have you been to your house yet?" Alexander asked.

Janie shook her head. "There's no point. It's gone."

She pointed in the distance to the part of town that had been the worst hit.

"You never know, you might find something in the rubble," he said.

Janie shook her head. "Not likely. From what I've seen in the videos and heard from people who have been able to get near there, there's nothing left to find." She gestured around the churchyard. "Not like here. They caught the fire before it crossed the road and hit the church and this part of town. Even though there's damage, at least much of it is salvageable." But as she said the words, she looked around the remains of her beautiful garden and her heart ached.

The firefighters had staged in the spot, and while she knew they had just been doing their job, it bothered her to see how carelessly they had trampled all over the rosebushes.

And yet, as soon as she thought it, she felt guilty. They had been doing their best, trying to save the town. How could she be worried about a few rosebushes when their loss had meant that so much of what she loved had been saved?

Alexander must have sensed her thoughts, because he put his arm around her. "This must have been a beautiful place," he said. "I know it won't be the same, but we can rebuild. I've seen memorials built in other parts of the state where they had destructive fires.

Maybe we could build a memorial of our gratitude that no lives were lost."

He must think her a terrible person for being so upset over the loss of such a seemingly trivial place.

"This was my mother's favorite spot."

Alexander pulled her closer to him. "You've told me that. I'm sure it makes your loss feel even worse. I hope I didn't sound too insensitive to your grief. I can't imagine how difficult it is for you to be grieving your mother and dealing with this at the same time."

It was strange, accepting comfort from him. From anyone. Janie was used to being the strong one. As wrong as it felt to have Alexander's arm around her, she also didn't want him to let go.

"Thank you," she said. "It's strange, because in all the loss that this town is suffering now, my mother's passing seems like such a small thing."

Her voice wavered and she could feel the tears wetting her eyes. She shouldn't have gone there. She needed to have all her faculties so she could help with the cleanup effort.

Alexander pulled her into a tight hug. "You don't always have to be strong. While you're not the only one who's lost something here, it doesn't make what you have lost insignificant."

His words gave her permission to do the thing she hadn't allowed herself to do since her nightmares began.

Janie sobbed.

It wasn't those pretty sobs that you see on television where the woman's makeup still looks perfect and you wonder if she was really sad at all. She sounded like a braying cow, and she wanted to make herself stop, but she couldn't.

Her mother was dead. Her house had burned down. The town was virtually destroyed.

She tried to pull away, but Alexander held her tighter. "Let it out. You've been strong for everyone else, and now it's your turn."

The trouble with Alexander not having grown up in this town was that he didn't understand it was her job to be strong for everyone else. Everyone counted on her. They needed her. Especially with her mom gone.

She just couldn't bring herself to break free from his grasp to tell him that.

So she stood there, crying in Alexander's arms. And after what felt like hours, her tears slowed, her sobs subsided and her grip on him loosened.

He gave her a tiny squeeze and whispered in her ear, "It's going to be okay."

It seemed almost ridiculous to believe him, except she did. Janie pulled away and nodded. He took a handkerchief out of his pocket and handed it to her.

"Here."

He waved it at her like he didn't want to tell her how badly she needed it. But she knew she looked a mess.

As she took it, she laughed. "Are you implying that the raccoon look isn't a good one for me?"

Alexander smiled and shook his head. "I would never imply that a lady is looking less than beautiful, when a woman's true beauty is in her heart." Then he gave a small smile. "And if I were to judge you in that way, well…" He turned away, like he was embarrassed.

"I can't tell if you were trying to pay me a compliment or not," Janie said.

Alexander looked back at her. "I did intend to pay a compliment, but then I realized that's not appropriate, given the circumstances. So I'm sorry. I didn't mean to offend you. I was just trying to be nice."

The way he stumbled over his words softened her heart toward him. It had been a long time since a man had complimented her like that. Sure, Ty and some of the other guys she'd grown up with would say things to her from time to time, but that was different. They were friends, and they'd known her forever.

Even though he'd stammered over it, and tried to dismiss it, Janie had to admit that it felt good to have someone who saw her this way. It didn't mean it would go anywhere, of course, but she'd forgotten what it was like to be admired by a man.

Sam's dad had been full of compliments back when they were dating. He'd been almost too effusive in his praise. Janie should have known that he hadn't been sincere, but back in college, it had been the first time since anyone had ever seen her as more than just one of the gang. Or worse, as the untouchable pastor's daughter.

She could tell Alexander was trying to do his best. Tears filled her eyes again as she realized just how starved she'd been for such genuine appreciation.

She smiled at him. "It's okay. It's kind of nice. Sometimes you get lost in the world of being a mom and serving others."

The way he was looking at her, she wondered if she'd said too much. She sounded like a total dork. Or worse, desperate.

"I'm sorry." She took a step back and turned toward the church. "We should probably check on my father. I know he wanted to be alone for a moment to survey the damage, but I know he shouldn't do this completely alone."

She didn't wait for his response, but strode in the direction of the church.

While the church hadn't burned, the smoke around it had caused so much damage, it would be a while before they could hold services there.

Ricky had let everyone use his lodge yesterday for church, and many of the neighbors whose barns were still standing had come together to offer theirs up as well. While it wasn't an ideal situation, Janie couldn't help thinking that this was what church was supposed to look like. Everyone who was able shared what they had for the good of the community.

When she entered the church, Alexander hung back.

Had she scared him off with her weird comment about enjoying his compliment?

This was why she didn't date or get involved romantically with anyone.

Janie stopped. Wait. What was she thinking? Going from accepting a compliment to considering dating him? That was just too weird. Obviously, the fire and her grief had gotten to her. Poor Alexander was here on a difficult mission of his own. Rather than connecting with his long-lost family, he had been helping the community deal with the fire. Janie had spent more time with him than he had with his new family. And now, he was here for her. He didn't need this kind of complication in his life. And really, she didn't, either.

Janie found her father in the chapel, examining the broken cross that had always stood at the front of the altar.

Janie stood beside her father. "It can be fixed," she said.

Her father shook his head. "It won't be the same."

She slipped her hand into his. "That's not what the man who raised me used to say. Do you remember the story you told me about how the Japanese would put gold into cracks in porcelain to make it even more beautiful? Is this not the same thing?"

Her father put his arm around her. "You're right. But it just seems like so much all at once."

She squeezed him back. "We'll get through it. No matter what troubles have ever come our way, you've always told me that God would bring us through stronger than we were."

He pulled her close and hugged her. "I know you're right. And if anyone came to me with a list of the problems that we face, I would tell them the same thing. But it seems so much harder without Bette by my side."

They hadn't spoken much of their shared grief. They'd been so busy preparing for the funeral, and now dealing with the fire, that this was the first he'd spoken of his loss.

"I know," Janie said. "I need her, too. There's so much I want to talk to her about. And I want to just sit with her for a moment."

Her father squeezed her tight. "What are we going to do?" he asked. "I know God will get us through this. I just hadn't expected it to be so much all at once."

Then he looked up at her. "I keep asking myself what your mother would do, but I can't get to the answer because I miss her so much."

Janie pulled away and gestured at the broom closet. "You know what she would do. Let's see how much of this mess we can get cleaned up before they kick us out."

Her father brushed his tears away with the back of his sleeve and nodded. "You're right. I can picture her now, rolling her eyes at me for being so stupid and not seeing the obvious."

He chuckled and shook his head. "She was a good woman. I see a lot of her in you. We've been too busy to talk much the past few days, but I hope you know just how proud of you she would be."

Tears filled her eyes at his words. "I know I've disappointed you in the past, like when I got pregnant. I'm trying to do better."

Unexpectedly, he pulled her into his arms again, giving her a tight hug and kissing her on top of the head. "You have never been a disappointment. Yes, it was hard when you came back from school, pregnant and alone. But it turned you into the woman you are today, and it gave me my grandson, so I'm not disappointed at all."

Something about his words opened up a wound in her heart she hadn't realized hadn't fully healed. Tears flowed down her face. "I still feel like everyone judges me for what I did."

Her father gave her another squeeze, then pulled away, staring at her intently. "You judge yourself more than anyone else has. You've proven your integrity time and again.

You chose to trust the wrong man, but that doesn't have to be the shame you live under forever. God has forgiven you. We have forgiven you. So maybe it's time to forgive yourself."

She hadn't thought of it that way. True, there had been a lot of whispers when she first came back to town. And yes, initially her parents had questioned her. But she had to admit that no one had said anything negative about her recently.

A noise at the back of the church caught her attention. Alexander. He'd asked about Sam's father, as many did, but the more she thought about it, the more she realized he hadn't been judging her. He'd just been curious.

She turned back to her father. "You may be right," she said. "It's obviously something I need more healing on."

Janie started to go toward the utility closet to grab the broom, but her father stopped her. "I hope you get it. It pains me to think that you are living under the shame of something that happened years ago, that you've repented of and that God has granted his forgiveness for. You're free. If you let yourself be."

Tears stung the back of her eyes as she nodded and took a deep breath to calm down. "Thank you. But we have a lot of work to do if we're going to get this church back up and running."

Her father shook his head slowly and chuckled. "You are your mother's daughter."

When she went to the closet and grabbed the broom, Alexander was right there.

"Can I help?" he asked.

The hesitation in his voice made her realize he wasn't just asking about the cleanup. She'd already fallen apart in his arms once today, and she wasn't ready for a repeat. Everyone counted on Janie to hold it together. Her father had just said it himself. She was her mother's daughter. No one would have ever accused Bette Roberts of being weak. It was Janie's job to take care of everyone, just like her mother had. And even though what she really wanted to do most right now was crawl up in her bed with a cuddly blanket and cry until she had no more tears left, that wasn't going to help anyone else in this town recover from the devastating fire.

She grabbed the broom and handed it to Alexander. "You take the left side, and I'll take the right. We'll get it done in no time."

He stared at the broom, then at her. He opened his mouth, clearly wanting to say something, but then closed it as he shook his head slowly. "All right. Let's do this."

The smile he gave her told her that he understood. Maybe he did want to comfort her further, but he seemed to understand that wasn't what she needed right now. And he seemed to accept that.

She resisted the urge to hug him as he gave her a rough smile and turned to go to the other side of the church. He didn't know it yet, and it wasn't an emotion she wanted to explore, but God had brought him into her life for a reason.

It felt wrong to Alexander, intruding on this moment between father and daughter. But one of the firemen had needed to talk to Pastor Roberts, and Alexander had gone in to get him. He hadn't meant to eavesdrop. But hearing the sadness in Janie's voice as she talked about the past and her unexpected pregnancy brought even more shame to Alexander.

He'd spent the past few days working closely with her. Nothing about their interaction could convince him that she was the mercenary she had been painted as. There had to be a reasonable explanation for her actions. But how was he supposed to find it? How could he get her to open up to him? And how was he supposed to do it in the middle of all this activity?

Once again, it seemed wrong to take advantage of the situation.

When Janie went to the broom closet, it gave him the opportunity he'd been looking for. After telling the pastor that he was wanted, Alexander went to the closet.

"Can I help?" he'd asked, grabbing one of the brooms. It felt good to be useful. To some extent, he understood why Janie had been working so hard and keeping busy. It was easier to stay busy to take his mind off the troubling things in his heart.

As they fell into the rhythm of sweeping the interior of the church, he found comfort in the work. Funny, he'd never felt the same at his job. Even though he'd always justified his hours at the desk as being the means to an end, something that would be helpful to others in the future, he hadn't found so much satisfaction in it as he did in these simple tasks like sweeping the floor.

He'd never seen the value in menial work, other than something he needed to get done. But now, it seemed to be something more. He paused at the end of the row and turned to see Janie, who had stopped sweeping for a moment to hug an elderly woman. He'd watched her hug a lot of people the past few days, her generous giving spirit warming his heart.

Until earlier in the churchyard, he hadn't seen her receive comfort from anyone else. Something stuck in his throat at remembering that moment. He'd never felt so useful. Wanted. Needed. Like he connected with her in a more meaningful way than he'd ever connected with anyone else.

He wasn't supposed to like her. But when he tried hard to see her as the villain, she would do something sweet and heroic like comfort this elderly woman, and he couldn't reconcile it with what he'd been told about her.

This was why having a menial task like cleaning up the mess in the sanctuary was a welcome relief from everything troubling him. But just as he began sweeping again, Janie and the old lady approached him.

"Mrs. Peterson, this is Alexander. He's the one who helped me rescue your horses and dog, and he also had the presence of mind to grab your scrapbooks."

Before he could respond, the old lady had wrapped her arms around him, giving him a squeeze tighter than he would have thought her frail body capable of.

"Bless you, dear boy. My sister Elaine sent

them to me to look at, and when she heard about the fire, she berated me for letting a family treasure get lost. But it wasn't lost, thanks to you."

All the while, the older woman kept hugging him and smiling at him as tears rolled down her cheeks.

Yes, he'd sensed they were important. But he hadn't known just how much that small action would mean to this woman.

Even though he had never considered himself much of a hugger, he found himself squeezing the old woman back.

"It was my pleasure. I'm just glad I saw them. I can't imagine what other treasures you must have lost. I wish I could have done more."

Mrs. Peterson released him, then turned to smile at Janie. "You got everything. Janie took the safe from my room as well as our wedding picture. And all my animals are safe. Everything else is just stuff. I have the things that mean the most to me, and that's what matters."

He'd heard much of the same over the past few days. Stuff could be replaced, but people couldn't, and the blessing they were all thanking God the most for was that no lives had been lost. Even the local ranchers had all managed to get the livestock to safety.

"I did what anyone would do," he told her honestly. "I'm glad I could help."

Before Mrs. Peterson could respond, his cell phone rang. He didn't have to look at it to know who was calling. It was the senator's ring tone.

A reminder that as much as Alexander wanted to be a part of this community, he had bigger issues at stake.

Chapter Five

"I'm sorry," Alexander told the ladies. "This is an important call I need to take."

As he walked away, he answered the phone. "Hello."

The senator didn't return his greeting, but instead jumped right in. "Well? Do you have her signature yet?"

Alexander stepped out of the building to give himself more privacy and surveyed the area around him. This town was completely devastated, and the senator wanted results that had nothing to do with the tragedy.

"It's complicated," Alexander said. "I'm sure you've seen it on the news. Almost her entire town has burned down. I've been helping with the rescue and relief efforts. She's been equally busy with them, and there hasn't been time to sit down and talk about the agreement."

The senator made a frustrated noise. "I didn't ask you to go there to do relief efforts. I asked you to get a signature."

Clearly, the senator didn't understand how important this was. Maybe the news media was underestimating the amount of damage that had been done. "With all due respect, sir, the situation here is quite bad. Even if I weren't helping with the relief efforts, she is. So how do I take her away from something vital to her community, especially about something that she doesn't want to talk about? She's already thrown out your investigator, and as you said, it's a delicate matter. She refuses to talk about the past, so it's going to take time to get her to open up."

There was silence on the other end for a moment—maybe the senator was looking up the news reports so he could see for himself.

"Maybe I chose the wrong person for the job. I was told you could get results. Where are your results?"

Unbelievable. This community had just suffered a catastrophic fire, and all the senator cared about was a signature to keep Janie from talking about something she wasn't inclined to talk about anyway.

"I don't think she's as much of a threat as you perceive her to be," Alexander said. "I have given her every opening possible to bad-mouth your son, and she's refused to do so. She refuses even to say his name. If I didn't know the full story from you, I would be completely in the dark about her situation. You're barking up the wrong tree."

"She's gotten to you, hasn't she?" The anger in the senator's voice was more intense than Alexander had expected. "She's a seductress, that one. Seems so sweet and kind, wears a mask to make everyone believe she's completely innocent. But let me assure you, she is a viper."

So the senator had been saying. But as Alexander turned to make sure no one was within earshot, he saw Janie walking Mrs. Peterson to her car. She was no viper. But he'd also seen the evidence from the senator about everything she'd done. Once again, he wondered how to reconcile the two sides of the story.

"She hasn't tried anything with me. She's made it very clear that she doesn't date. Again, though she has been given plenty of opportunities and openings to discuss the past, she has staunchly refused. She's not a threat."

"So long as I keep making her payments," the senator said. "But what then? What happens when she demands more money?"

He had a point, and it was one Alexander had been thinking about a lot. Though he'd prayed that she wouldn't lose her house in the fire, she had. She did have insurance, though the insurance adjusters said it would take time to process the claims. He wasn't sure what Janie would do. She'd admitted to him that her job working for the community resource center had ended, but now, with the local elementary school also lost in the fire, everyone who worked at the school was faced with their jobs being in limbo. Her part-time job was gone, and now her full-time job possibly no longer existed.

Not that Janie had mentioned it to him. But he had been talking to one of the local teachers, who wasn't sure how everything was going to be handled. They were having an emergency school board meeting later in the week, so until then, no one had answers.

Would this drive Janie to enough desperation to ask the senator for more money?

"I think we need to wait and see a little longer," Alexander said. "With the fire, everyone's financial situation is precarious. Let's see if she asks for more money. If she does, we can use that as the leverage we need to get her to sign. If she doesn't, then I think we let it go. She's not a threat."

"In politics, we don't wait and see. That's a loser's game. All it would take is my opponent finding Janie, talking to her and offering her more money before she has a chance to go to me. No, you've got to get her to sign now. The election might be a year away, but we have to be prepared."

Janie was coming toward him, which meant he didn't have much more time.

"With all due respect, sir, does anyone know she exists?"

There was a brief silence, then the senator said, "I don't believe so. But that doesn't mean they won't find out. And if they do, it could ruin us."

Janie had stopped to talk to another person getting ready to enter the church. Over the past few days, he'd seen no sign of her being as greedy as the senator said.

"I don't think pressuring her is the right answer. You tried that, and it backfired. I'll spend more time here, trying to get close enough to her to get a signature. I'll also know if someone from your opponent's side is poking around. As you said when you sent me, I have reason to be here. None of them do. If I see anyone, we can rethink our strategy."

The strained silence made Alexander wonder just how angry he'd made the senator with his suggestion. People didn't talk back to him. They said, "yes, sir," and did exactly what he asked.

"My investigator did say that Janie was difficult. If you scare her too much, she's liable to go to the other side to get back at me. We'll try it your way. See if this tragedy makes her ask for more money. If she does, we'll use it as leverage to get her to sign. But if she doesn't, you will remain in play, keeping watch and looking for an opportunity to get her to sign."

It wasn't the answer he'd hoped for, but at least it was an answer. And at least it allowed him to remain here longer, and not just for Janie's sake.

He hadn't been lying when he'd said they'd all been too busy for him to talk much with her. He hadn't even gotten the chance to speak much with his biological family. Everyone had been busy, giving aid and doing what they could for the community. As it was, Alexander had given up the cabin he'd rented and was sleeping in a sleeping bag in the great room of Ricky's house, along with several other men who had been displaced by the fire or had given up their rooms or homes for those who needed them.

A nearby car door opened, and Sam, Janie's son, came barreling out toward him.

"Mr. Alexander. Mr. Alexander. Guess what?"

Sam didn't seem to notice Alexander was on the phone, and while Alexander hadn't spent much time with the little boy, he was often Janie's shadow, trailing her as she helped others.

"Hey, buddy. I'm on the phone. Give me just a second and you can tell me what has you so excited."

He turned his attention back to the call. "I'm sorry about that. As I said, things are crazy here, with the fire."

"Just get results," the senator said, then hung up.

It wasn't the best conversation he'd had with the senator, but at least he was willing to trust him and give him a little more time to make everything work.

Alexander shoved his phone back in his pocket and squatted down to eye level with the little boy. "What's up, buddy?"

Sam grinned. "Remember I told you about my favorite dump truck?"

Alexander didn't, but it wasn't for lack of paying attention. Everyone in this town had some favorite possession they'd been telling him about, and it was hard to keep them all straight.

Alexander smiled as Rachel came up behind them.

"I'm sorry, I saw you on the phone but couldn't stop him. Sam wasn't intruding, was he?"

Alexander shook his head. "No, I was just finishing up. But Sam here was telling me about his dump truck."

"The fireman wouldn't let me go to my house," Sam said. "He said it was too dangerous for little kids. But then Jed, one of the other firemen, the one who let us ride in the fire truck over the summer, told me he'd have a look around. And then he brought out my dump truck."

Rachel's daughter, Katie, had joined them, carrying the remains of a metal dump truck. It was misshapen, and worse for the wear, but you couldn't tell it by the smiles on the kids' faces.

"It's my dump truck, too," Katie said. "We saved up our allowances and joined them together to buy it."

Then she held it out to Sam. "I got to hold it for a while, so now it's your turn."

Sam grinned as he took the dump truck from Katie. Then he held it up for Alexander. "See? We're going to fix it up just like new."

Rachel looked at him like she wasn't sure what he was going to say, and that she hoped he would somehow find a way to be encouraging. He didn't blame her. The little boy had lost so much.

"I think, with a little bit of elbow grease, you could do something special with it," Alexander said.

Rachel made a little noise, like he'd said the wrong thing. He didn't have any experience with kids, but he was trying his best. Thankfully, Sam and Katie grinned.

"There was a story in the Bible," Sam said. "About these three guys with weird names. We learned about them in Sunday school. They were put in the fire to burn them, but God saved them, just like our dump truck."

Rachel made a noise. "That's Shadrach, Meshach and Abednego, and they came out of the fire completely unharmed."

The kids' faces fell, and for someone who seemed to think that Alexander wouldn't do a good job at explaining fire survival to the kids, she wasn't doing so hot herself.

"But I'm sure that God did give you your dump truck as a sign that the fire can't destroy everything," Alexander said. "Even though a lot of precious things to us were destroyed, we all have the stuff that matters the most, don't we?"

The kids both nodded, smiles filling their faces once more.

"That's what Mom says," Sam said. "You're smart, just like her."

Sam must've heard Janie's voice somewhere in the background, because at that moment the kids both turned to her.

"I've got to go show her my dump truck."

The kids took off running, leaving Rachel standing there with him. They hadn't spoken much since their first meeting, other than to share the logistical information necessary for working together on the relief efforts.

"I know," he said. "I probably didn't do the best job talking to them. But I'm not used to kids, and I'm doing my best."

Rachel shook her head. "No. It's okay. I wasn't doing so great myself. I was actually going to thank you for trying. You didn't sign up for any of this. You just wanted to meet Ricky and get closure on an uncomfortable piece of your family history. But you stayed. You jumped in when you could have easily left."

Rachel was making him sound like a hero. He wasn't, but he couldn't tell her that. Yes, he'd stayed because they needed the help. But he'd had another, more selfish reason for staying.

"I did what anyone would have done."

Rachel shook her head again. "Really? Not from where I'm standing. Ricky's ranch was booked solid with guests. Not a single one of them stayed to help with relief efforts. It's not what anyone would do."

He hadn't given a thought to any of Ricky's other guests. He'd just assumed that they were somehow taken care of.

"I appreciate what you're saying," he finally said. "But I'm not a hero. Not any more than every other person in this town working tirelessly to take care of everything."

Rachel nodded slowly. "All right. If that's how you want to play it, I respect that. I know I haven't exactly been friendly to you, and we haven't had much of a chance to talk. I was hurt by your rejection when you first found out about me, but now I can see that it probably was just as shocking for you and you didn't know how to process it. You needed time."

He hadn't noticed any hostility in her, and hadn't thought she was holding anything

against him. But before he could reassure
her of that fact, she continued.

"I always wanted a brother. It's crazy to
think that I have at least two. I know you're
mostly here for Ricky, but do you think you
could spend time getting to know your sister, too?"

The vulnerability in her voice made his
heart ache. Not just because of how she was
opening herself up to him, but because he felt
the same way about having a sister. The trouble was, as close as Rachel was to Janie, what
would Rachel do when he realized exactly
why Alexander was here? The two women
shared everything, and when Janie was evacuated, Rachel had opened up her home on the
ranch to her. Even though the cabin Rachel
shared with her husband and daughter was
small, they'd welcomed Janie and Sam into it.

"That would be nice," Alexander said. "I
know we have a long way to go. Taking care
of the community after the fire is the most
pressing issue right now. But I'll always be
available to talk, if you want to."

Maybe someday, after Rachel found out the
truth and hated him for a while, she would
look back on this conversation and understand that he truly did mean it when he said
he'd like to get to know her.

He'd have liked to say more, to give her something more reassuring, but the kids ran back to them, Janie in tow.

"I can't believe the dump truck survived the fire," Janie said.

"We prayed for it," Sam said, squaring his shoulders.

Katie mimicked his actions. "Yes we did. Now we have to go find Ryan to tell him about our dump truck."

The kids ran off to find their friend, Rachel following behind.

When they were alone, Janie smiled at him. "Thanks for what you said to Sam. One of the firefighters told him that the truck was junk he should throw out, and I know it looks rough, but having the truck means a lot to Sam. You made him feel good about it."

What was he supposed to say? That was the trouble with being here. Everyone kept complimenting him and telling him all these nice things, but he was just doing what he was supposed to do. People never thanked him like this at work. His coworkers hadn't hugged him when he'd realized they'd forgotten the campaign buttons for the fall parade and he'd gone out of his way to deliver them. Sure, it had been a hassle, but you did the right thing, even if it was a pain.

He tried to respond, but as soon as he opened his mouth, Janie shook her head at him. "No. Everyone gets on me about not being able to accept compliments, and I didn't understand it at first, but seeing you in action, I do. Stop telling people that what you're doing is nothing. Because to them, it's everything."

She looked at the ground and her voice softened. "It's not nothing."

Then she returned her gaze to him. "There aren't many men out there like you, and you need to know that what you did was special. To them, and to me."

It wasn't supposed to feel like this. Her words told him that he'd earned her trust. Which meant he should be able to talk to her about his reason for being here. But with the shy look in her eyes and the vulnerability in her spirit, he couldn't bring himself to do so.

She shifted her pose slightly and said, "Which is why I want to thank you for what you did in the garden. I don't do that with just anyone. But you're special. And you made me feel safe."

The look on her face told him that if he reached out and hugged her right now, she would fall into his arms and let him hold her, just like he had earlier in the garden. He was so close to accomplishing everything he wanted. And clearly, from the way the senator talked, this needed to be done sooner rather than later.

How could he hurt her?

He took a step back, then said, "I'm glad I could be there for you. I'll try to do better at accepting people's thanks and praise."

The light in Janie's eyes was almost too much for Alexander to take. He was trying to do the right thing, say the right thing, but her expression only made him feel even more uncomfortable.

"I can't be who you want me to be," he said. "Don't put me on any pedestals, because I guarantee you, I will fall."

His warning didn't dim the light in her eyes, and he hated himself for it. Why couldn't he say the right thing? He just needed her to understand that he wasn't who she thought he was. Not even close. She was building up this expectation of him that he could never meet. And he didn't know how to accomplish his objective while keeping both of their hearts safe.

Chapter Six

Though Janie would have liked to have talked more with Alexander, duty called. Now that the church had been cleared to allow people back in, it seemed like the whole town was filtering in, having checked their homes and seen the devastation. They needed a place to process everything.

The insurance adjusters had been out and were all crunching the numbers, trying to do the best they could. Though families would be getting checks to recover the lost possessions, other things had been lost that couldn't be so easily replaced.

Janie looked out across the church playground to the blackened remains of their town. People's homes were there, but also their businesses, their livelihood. Just a couple blocks away, she could see the remains of what used to be the elementary school.

To think that just a few days ago, she'd been upset at the loss of her part-time job at the community center. Now, her full-time one at the elementary school was also gone. It would take months, possibly even years, to rebuild all that had been lost. Half of the main business district was gutted. It was hard enough here, trying to stay in business, but with half of the people already struggling to keep their businesses afloat, what incentive did they have to rebuild?

Wiping the sweat off her brow, Janie paused at the end of the row of pews she'd been washing. Alexander had helped her carry them outside to clean. It seemed like she'd been scrubbing for hours, and none of it made a difference. She stood and stretched her back, and as she did so, Roger Huddleston, her next-door neighbor, approached.

"Janie. I'm so sorry. I grabbed a few things from your house and they're in my car, but I'm afraid I wasn't thinking very clearly, so I don't know if any of it will be of use to you."

He held up a vacuum. "I just bought this for Shelley's birthday last week. We don't have a house to vacuum anymore. Can the church use it?"

He laughed ruefully as he shook his head. "Why did I grab that vacuum? Sure, it had made Shelley so happy when I got it for her. But I wish I'd found a way to take her grandmother's china."

Janie stepped forward and hugged Roger. "We don't always think clearly in an emergency. Even though you didn't take Shelley's most prized possession, you did remember something she loved, and you wanted to do something nice for her."

He returned the hug, then turned to the door his wife was striding through.

"You tell *her* that."

Janie stepped forward and hugged her neighbor. "Shelley. I'm so glad to see you. Where are you guys staying?"

Shelley shrugged. "We threw everything we could into the camper, and we have it parked at a friend's house."

Then she looked over at the vacuum Roger was holding. "That stupid thing. Can you believe that's what he thought to pull out of the house?"

Janie shrugged. "His heart was in the right place. He was just telling me how it was a gift you'd really wanted, and it had made you happy. You guys lost a lot of precious things. But I hope you remember just how much

Roger loves you, and that when he grabbed the vacuum, it was because of that love."

Shelley smiled, then looked over at her husband. "It's true. I lost a lot of things in the fire, but I didn't lose the most important one."

Roger blushed, and it was sweet to see that a couple that had been together as long as Roger and Shelley could still share a moment like this. It reminded her a lot of her parents, and how Janie had wished she would find a love like that of her own.

Most of the time, she accepted it wasn't meant to be. But sometimes…

A noise on the other side of the church drew her attention. She turned to see Alexander helping an older lady with a load of boxes.

He was a good man, even though he seemed to protest the idea every time she brought it up. They hadn't had a lot of time to talk, like about what his plans were, how long he was saying and if he would be back.

She didn't blame him if he never came back. Imagine coming to meet your family, only to be thrust into a natural disaster. She'd heard him brush Rachel off when she'd complimented him for staying, just like he did whenever Janie made a big deal of something he'd done. It was amazing how much credit Alexander deserved, yet how little he accepted. He was such a good man. Janie wished that when she was younger, she'd pursued men because of their character, not because of the giddy feeling they put in her stomach. Though if she were honest, she would have to say that Alexander did both.

"That grandson of Ricky's is a fine young man," Shelley said. "The Ruiz genes run strong. I've never seen a man more eager to help others than Ricky. His grandson seems to be the same. What a blessing for him to come now when we need him most. Ricky must be so grateful to have him."

Janie nodded. "I'm grateful, too. He's been a big help around the church. He's done everything without complaint or even seeming weary. It's been so hard without my mom here, but Alexander has stepped up to help with so much of the work that the burden doesn't feel as heavy as it would otherwise."

Shelley gave her another hug. "So much loss in such a short time for your family. Bette was a dear friend, and she was very proud of you. I'm sure she would be proud of the work you're doing here."

Janie returned the hug and smiled at Shelley when she pulled away. "Thank you. It means a lot to hear that from one of her close friends. Your bunco group meant the world to her, and I'm so grateful for all your support."

The smile Shelley gave her was an affirmation that Janie needed to do a better job of accepting praise and comfort from others. And as she sent a quiet prayer, thanking God for His patience in teaching her this lesson, she felt a bit of the grief of losing her mother lift from her heart.

Shelley patted Janie's back then gestured around the churchyard. "This is a fine mess. I know the church usually hosts a Thanksgiving dinner for those who don't have a place to go, but with everything in disarray and needing cleaning, and half the town homeless, have you thought about what you're going to do? I'd offer my place, but—" Shelley gestured at the rubble in the area that was once their homes.

Janie hadn't even thought that far ahead. Sure, it was only a couple weeks away, but nothing about the season felt like Thanksgiving. Had the fire never happened, had her mother not died, the church would have been awash with harvest decorations and they would be planning the menu for their annual celebration.

Now, holding the event seemed nearly impossible.

"To be honest, I didn't think about it until now," Janie said. "I'm not even sure where to begin. Mom had a binder where she kept notes on all the church events and things she did. But I was reading it in bed the night before her funeral, trying to make sure I had every detail right, so I'm sure it's lost to us now."

Every single person who'd come to the church today had mourned the loss of a special possession. Each time, Janie thanked God that the things that had meant the most to her were all accounted for. But remembering the binder, and the fact that she hadn't put it on the list for people to get from her house, made her realize that she, too, had lost something irreplaceable.

Everything else she'd lost had been just stuff, covered by renter's insurance. The deputy watching her house during the funeral had been able to get the small safe with her important documents as well as the plastic tub with memorabilia, like Sam's baby book. She'd never imagined she'd ever have to use the fire plan she'd been taught at a fire safety meeting, but now she was glad she'd been prepared.

Fighting the tears threatening to overcome her, Janie looked back in the direction where she'd last seen Alexander. She knew that if she started crying now, Shelley would comfort her. And as much as she loved Shelley, it wasn't what Janie wanted.

Thankfully, Shelley seemed to sense that as she patted Janie kindly on the arm. "I'm so sorry. Many of us in the bunco group help your mother with the Thanksgiving dinner as well as other church activities. I'll talk to them and see what they remember. You don't have to do this alone. Your mother didn't."

For the first time, Janie realized that as much as she had always admired her mother's strength and fortitude, Shelley was right. She hadn't done this alone. How many times had Janie walked into the house to see her mother and her friends making decorations or preparing food for a church event? The bunco group had been the ones to throw Janie a baby shower and make sure that Sam had everything he needed. Even when her mother got sick, Shelley and her crew took turns relieving Janie and her father and spending time with her mother.

Not only had Janie's mother not been alone, Janie hadn't either.

She started to open her mouth to express her gratitude to Shelley, but Ricky approached.

"I heard you guys were parking your trailer at the O'Learys'. If you ever want more space, we can make room for you at the ranch," Ricky said.

"Thank you," Shelley said. "We're doing just fine for now, but you can check with Roger just in case."

As Ricky nodded, an idea came to Janie. "I hate to impose on you further, even though I know you say that helping the community isn't an imposition, but talking to Shelley made me realize that our town is in more need than ever for our annual Thanksgiving dinner."

Gesturing at the church, Janie continued, "As much as I would love to have it here, I don't think it will be ready in time. Do you have space at the ranch?"

A wide grin filled Ricky's face. "Of course. You know that your mother started that tradition with my Rosie, right? Thanksgiving was Rosie's favorite holiday, and she used to love planning the church celebration with Bette."

"That's right," Shelley said. "It's the whole reason Bette always insisted on making her special brownies for Thanksgiving. They were Rosie's favorite."

Alexander joined them as well. "Is everything all right, Janie? I saw you looking over at me a couple of times like you needed something."

One more thing to like about Alexander. He always seemed so in tune with her and her needs. Though he kept doing his best to warn her off, moments like these made her like him even more.

"Yes," she said. "We were talking about Thanksgiving, and the fact that the church always has a celebration. We can't have it here this year, and my mother's binder with all the information on what she does to organize it is lost in the fire, but Ricky has offered to host, and Shelley said that she and the bunco group would gather the information they remember because they helped my mother with all the events."

Alexander looked confused. "That's great. But what do you need me for?"

"To give her a hand, of course," Ricky said. "You two make a great team, and everyone has been commenting on what a bang-up job you do together."

She knew that look in Ricky's eyes. He thought he was playing matchmaker. Usually at this point, Janie would have groaned and commented on how she didn't need Ricky interfering in her life. But as she stole another glance at Alexander, she had to admit she wouldn't mind working closely with him and getting to know him better.

"It's settled, then," Shelley said. "We'll have the annual Thanksgiving celebration at the ranch. Me and the gals will be available to help you guys in any way we can. I'll start talking to people to get an idea of how many will come. Last year we had about 125, which is pretty normal. But with the fire, I'm not sure."

They made plans to get together later in the week at Ricky's to figure out what needed to be done. And even though Janie had been feeling good about being useful in cleaning up the church, having a more concrete, meaningful goal for the short term energized her in a way that cleaning the pews hadn't.

Ricky and Shelley wandered off to talk to Roger, but Alexander hung back.

"Are you sure you're okay?" he asked. "You looked kind of upset when you were talking to Shelley."

Most people didn't notice things like that about her. No one saw that when she said she was fine, she sometimes wasn't. Well, okay, that wasn't entirely true. Rachel often called her out on it, as did her friends at Three Sisters Ranch.

But men never noticed.

Which was why she couldn't give her standard answer to Alexander.

"Shelley was one of my mom's best friends." Janie explained about the binder, as well as the friendship of the ladies in the bunco group, and Alexander listened, nodding and murmuring in the appropriate places.

And she found it very comforting to pour her heart out to this man and not feel like she was imposing on him. Very comforting indeed.

Alexander couldn't wrap his head around the way this community was coming together after the fire. They'd spent the day of the fire with rescue efforts, then getting people settled in temporary places to stay. And now, everyone was working together to help the community start over and rebuild.

But as he looked at the people in the churchyard, checking in with one another and sharing their stories of what did and didn't survive the fire, he couldn't help wondering why the media wasn't giving this more attention. Why people like the senator weren't here to survey the damage for themselves. When he'd spoken with him earlier, the man had dismissed Alexander's comments about the devastation like he was talking about a fly in the room.

When it was Alexander's turn to run for office, he wouldn't forget about the people of Columbine Springs.

As if he could.

Janie was locking up for the night, and people were slowly heading to their cars and off to wherever they were staying. For some, it was an overcrowded house, with people who had lost everything. And for others, it was a temporary place until they could figure out where they were going next.

Janie came to stand beside him. "Are you ready to go home?"

Home. He wasn't sure what that word meant anymore. His townhome in Denver was the place he called home, but as he'd interacted with people whose homes had been lost, Alexander had to admit it was just a place to lay his head. The ranch? Ricky had told him it was his home, but he couldn't feel comfortable there, not with his secret mission in the back of his mind.

But he turned to Janie and said, "Yes. Did you get everything done that you needed to?"

Janie shrugged. "Everything? Not by a long shot. But it's progress. I've got some things I need to bring back to the ranch. Can you help me carry them out to the truck?"

Ricky had let Alexander borrow one of the ranch trucks. His car remained parked next to the church, and while it had survived the fire, the smoke damage was another issue. An insurance adjuster would be by in the coming week to look at it, but until then, it needed to remain where it was because the smoke smell inside was too unbearable to handle. He was glad he'd thought to at least grab his briefcase and wallet. Everything else might be a loss, but he had the most important things for his mission.

"Of course. You know I'm here to help," Alexander said.

"I just wanted to say—" Janie hesitated, like she was treading on uncertain ground.

"I don't want to talk about it," he said.

"You don't even know what I was going to say."

"I'm sorry," he said. "I know I said I'd do better about accepting praise for my work, but I'm tired, and it's been a long day."

She reached over and touched his arm. "I understand. But that's not entirely what I wanted to talk about. I mean, yes, what you've been doing here is a big deal. But I feel bad that you came here for one purpose, and you've spent so little time with your family so far. It must be frustrating for you not to get to know them because you're spending all your time helping me. I wanted you to know how much that sacrifice meant to me."

Except that he was fulfilling his purpose. That was the part she'd missed. The part he couldn't tell her.

But even worse was that same light shining in her eyes that he'd seen earlier. He was grateful he was driving, because it would've been so easy for him to take her into his arms.

"Maybe it's not a sacrifice," he said. "Maybe I'm nervous about being around them and I don't know what to say or how to feel. And just like all this busywork is keeping you distracted from your feelings about losing your mother, maybe it's doing the same for me."

She murmured, as though she agreed. Giving his arm another squeeze, she said, "You don't have to be afraid of them. Surely by now you've seen for yourself what good people they are."

Yes, but that was the problem. The more he grew to like everyone here, the harder it was to remain focused on a mission that would surely hurt Janie.

"What do you need me to bring out to the truck?" he asked.

He took a step toward the Sunday School area, where they'd been sorting things most of the day, but Janie stopped him.

"At some point, you're going to have to deal with the difficult emotions about your family."

Alexander turned to look at her. "And what if that's not what I'm afraid of? You think you know me, but you don't. You're trying so hard to psychoanalyze me and figure me out, but there's a lot about me you don't know. Stop trying to fix me. There are so many other things happening right now that you are one hundred percent capable of fixing, but I'm not one of them."

The wounded look on her face was exactly why he didn't want to have this conversation. Why every deep conversation with Janie was difficult. He couldn't share his feelings with her. And he couldn't let her count on him to share hers.

"You're right, I don't know you. There's so much I don't know about you, and every time I try to get to know you, you shut me down. I don't know your favorite color, your favorite food, what you like to do for fun. I don't even know if you're married or not."

Her own words seemed to startle her as she removed her hand from his arm and scooted back on the seat. "Is that it? Are you afraid you're betraying someone else? If so, you should just tell me."

He should tell her he was single. Was it possible that something could grow between them, and he could use that to get her to trust him enough to find a solution that would work with the senator?

But doing so would probably ruin his hope of getting to work with the senator in Washington, a plum position for someone with his aspirations. The senator already thought he was falling for Janie, and as a result, he didn't trust Alexander's judgment as fully as he should.

Why did this have to be so difficult?

He glanced over Janie, and she scooted away, like she was bracing herself for his rejection.

"I'm not married," he said. "But I have a life back in Denver. And while I've taken time off to be here, at some point I have to go back to my life, my family."

Her body relaxed slightly. "It's funny, you never did tell me exactly what you do. You keep dodging the question. Are you a criminal or something?"

Alexander laughed. "I guess it probably seems like that. But no."

He'd been cagey because he didn't know how to explain what he did without revealing the truth. But he owed her something.

"I work as an advisor to a wealthy and powerful man. Most of what I do is covered by a nondisclosure agreement, and while I can safely say that I've never done anything illegal as part of my job, and neither has my boss, I also have to be careful about what I say because I don't want to violate that agreement, and I don't have his permission to talk about it."

The truth. A freeing thing. Everything he'd just said was true. All of the senator's employees signed nondisclosure agreements. But he still felt guilty about the parts he could technically tell her, except that it would ruin everything.

"I understand," she said. "I think. It's so weird, how until recently I hadn't heard anything about nondisclosure agreements. And now they seem to be everywhere. It's like the world is changed, but I haven't changed with it."

Was this the opening he'd been looking for?

He turned more toward her and scooted a little bit closer. "I wouldn't say that. Nondisclosure agreements aren't all that common.

Just when you're dealing with a secretive line of work. Where else have you heard it recently?"

She hesitated, like she wanted to tell him, so he nodded encouragingly but she shook her head.

"It doesn't matter. I just…"

For a moment, Janie looked like she was about to cry again. Then she said, "I used to talk to my mom about all these things. Well, not all of them, and that's what I wish I could take back. I wish I had just been honest with her from the very beginning. Not that I lied. But I've kept a lot of secrets. And now that she's gone and I desperately need someone to talk to who will understand, I feel so alone."

God hadn't been one for answering any of the prayers he'd uttered so far, and maybe it was because he still wasn't sure what he believed in that area, but he knew God loved Janie, so he prayed that his next move wouldn't be a mistake.

He held an arm out to her. "You don't have to be alone if you don't want to. I promise, I won't judge you for your secrets. Maybe it would be freeing for you to tell the truth to someone who doesn't have all the past baggage of expectations. I'm here for you, if you'll let me be."

She took a step toward him, but then she stopped. "Trust goes both ways. I understand you not wanting to violate your nondisclosure agreement. I respect that, and I'm glad you finally explained that to me. But you and I both know there's a whole lot more that you aren't opening up to me about. So I'm going to trust you with my secrets, then you have to trust me with yours."

Janie had him there.

"I can't," he said. "There's so much you don't understand. I wish I could. If I were to open up to anyone in this world, it would be you. But I can't."

Janie nodded slowly. "I understood when you told me you were bound by a nondisclosure agreement. Give me a little credit."

Could he lay all his cards out about his real reason for being here?

"Maybe we take this one step at a time. I just trusted you with something that I haven't told anyone else here. Maybe you can trust me with just one of your secrets."

For a moment, she looked like she was considering his idea. "All of my secrets revolve around one big one. And I'm not ready to share that, with you or anyone."

Alexander took a deep breath. "Is it about Sam's father?"

She stared at him, a shocked expression on her face. "What makes you say that?"

He shrugged. "Because you shut down every time it comes up. Why are you so afraid to reveal who he is?"

Janie bit her lip, hesitation in her eyes. "When I told him I was keeping the baby, he threatened me. He didn't want to be a father, and when I tried to appeal to his family for help, they made it clear they wanted nothing to do with Sam or me. They threatened me that if I ever revealed who Sam's father was, they would destroy me."

That wasn't exactly how the senator had said how it went. And if Janie was so afraid of them, why was she blackmailing them?

"Why do you think they would destroy you?"

The fear in her eyes was real as she responded, "Because they said so. That's where I heard about the nondisclosure agreement recently. They want me to sign one, preventing me from ever saying who Sam's father is."

Now they were getting somewhere. "Why don't you?" he asked. "It's not like you told anyone. Are they offering anything in exchange for your signature?"

Janie nodded. "A lot of money, actually. When I said no, they told me to name my price. I don't even know what I would do with the money they offered me, let alone more."

Was it going to be this easy? "So why not take it? People were talking about how the community center was losing its funding, so you weren't going to have a part-time job anymore, and with the elementary school burning down... Well, you haven't complained about your circumstances, but based on what everyone else is saying about their situation, it's not hard to glean that things are going to be very difficult for you. It seems like a no-brainer to take the offer, especially if it's so much money."

The look Janie gave him could have melted everything the fire didn't. "You don't get it," she said. "I don't want anything from him. He's made it clear where we stand, and it feels wrong to take anything from him now. I get that he wants to buy me off. But I refuse to put a price on my integrity."

She pointed at a stack of boxes. "Those need to go to the ranch. Hopefully it will supplement the things people got from the Red Cross."

A stuffed bunny peeked out from the top of one of the boxes. Once again, Alexander thought about how much everyone had lost, and how precious such a small item would be to a child.

He understood the value of integrity. It was something he held dear, and the more time he spent with Janie, the more he understood how important it was to her. Which was why they were both here, gathering items like this toy so that people who'd lost so much could find hope.

Where was the hope for them in this situation?

"I understand the idea of not compromising your integrity," Alexander said. "But I also believe that a father should support his child. If it's true that Sam's father has never paid a dime of child support, don't you think you could at least accept that?"

Janie sighed, but he didn't know if it was out of frustration that he was pushing the issue, or if maybe she was starting to break.

"For years, I'd hoped for child support. I would have done anything to get him to pay something. I even thought it would be nice for him to have a relationship with Sam. I didn't have money for a lawyer, and when my letters to him were returned unopened, I figured this was God's way of telling me to let it go. God has fought my battles for me, and I will continue to let him do so."

The hesitation in her voice made him wonder if that's what she believed, or if it was what she'd been telling herself to make excuses for Bucky's actions.

"And what if this is God's way of providing? Maybe God knew that you were going to lose everything, including your job, and he gave this to you as a gift?"

Janie shook her head. "I don't think so. It's dirty money. The only reason he's offering it to me is because he wants me to sign a paper saying I will never reveal who Sam's father is. Sam already has so many questions, but he's too young to understand the answers. He deserves to hear the truth someday."

On one hand, she had a point. Alexander knew that under the terms of the agreement, Janie was prohibited from telling Sam who his father was. The senator didn't want the boy coming out of the woodwork sometime in the future, when he had more at stake, and ruining everything for the senator.

But on the other hand, it wasn't like the senator would ever acknowledge Sam or have a relationship with him. It seemed silly to pass up money for something that was going to happen anyway.

"So tell him the truth. Tell him that his father didn't want anything to do with him, and he didn't want his identity revealed."

Janie shook her head. "I can't take away his right to the truth. That doesn't sound fair. Think about what you're going through. How it felt to realize you'd been lied to all this time. How hurtful would it be for him to know that I sold out his right to the truth?"

He hadn't thought of it that way. But he wasn't asking Janie to lie to Sam.

"That's different. You haven't lied to him. And surely it would be better for you to be the one to tell him that his father wants nothing to do with him than for him to show up on his doorstep and be rejected."

"Maybe," Janie said. "But I can't take that choice away from him. You made the choice to find your biological family, even though you had a family who loved you. You came here even though it made your family angry, and your brother has chosen not to do the same. Who knows what will happen if Sam decides he wants to meet his father fifteen, twenty years down the line? Maybe his father will be more receptive. Or maybe he won't. While he's a child, I can make decisions for him, but I need the door open for him to choose when he's an adult."

Alexander couldn't see a world in which

the senator or Bucky would want anything to do with Sam. They already felt so strongly about that. Sam represented a mistake that the family would not and could not acknowledge. It would ruin the senator's career. But he couldn't tell her that.

The strained look on Janie's face told Alexander he'd pushed too far. Too hard.

"I'm sorry," Alexander said. "I just thought maybe it would be a possible solution to your financial troubles."

Janie's expression softened. "I know. You spent the past few days fixing everyone else's problems, so you would naturally want to help with mine. But trust me, it's not the solution."

She hesitated, then continued. "Please don't tell anyone about this. You're the only person I've told about the nondisclosure agreement, and this is the most I've told anyone about Sam's father. It's not something I talk about."

The vulnerability on her face convinced him there was no way she could be blackmailing the senator. He held his arms out to her. "I won't. Thank you for trusting me." But the words felt hollow in his heart. This was what he'd been trying to do all along. Get her to trust him about Sam's father. Give him the opportunity to convince her to sign the nondisclosure agreement. But hearing the conviction in her voice and the pain in her words, he wasn't sure this was the right thing to do anymore.

Someone was blackmailing the senator, that he knew for sure.

But if not Janie, then who? And how? He'd seen the documentation. While he wanted to believe there was a rational explanation, he couldn't come up with one. And as Janie moved to accept his hug, Alexander wondered whose side he was on anymore.

The senator could do good things for the country, for everyone. But Alexander disagreed with how he was handling the Janie situation, especially now that Alexander had gotten to know her.

So who was he supposed to betray? His country? Or the woman he was growing to care for more and more every day?

Chapter Seven

Janie had thought that unburdening herself about Sam's father would make her feel better. But since her drive with Alexander a couple of days ago, she'd only felt more unsettled. Was he right? As she trudged out of the high school from the impromptu board meeting to determine what they were going to do with the children from the elementary school, her friend Erin came up to her and put her arm around her. "I'm so sorry about your job," she said. "It doesn't seem fair that you have to lose it."

The school board had decided the elementary school children would have classes at the high school. They'd combined various classrooms, and would be using some older, unused space to accommodate everyone for the time being.

Janie shrugged. "It wasn't unexpected. Even though they need aides in some of the classes at the high school, there isn't enough room for all of us. I get it. They promised that once the new elementary school is built, those of us being let go will have first priority on the jobs."

The concern on Erin's face was touching. "But what will you do in the meantime? You have a son to raise."

Janie shrugged. "I'll figure it out. I always have. They're giving us a severance package, so I'm not totally destitute."

It sounded a lot better than it felt. Especially because the kids were going to be crammed into larger class sizes, due to space restrictions. Which meant learning was going to be even more difficult for Sam than it already was. She couldn't afford his reading therapy with the two jobs she'd had. So where did that leave her? More importantly, where did it leave Sam?

She hugged Erin goodbye, then started toward the ranch truck she'd been driving. The insurance company had decided it would cost more to get the smoke damage to her car repaired than it would to get her an entirely new car. She was still waiting on them to process the paperwork, but even then, that meant a drive to the city to purchase a new car. She wasn't sure where she'd find the time to do that, but Ricky had been generous in allowing her, and anyone else who had need, the use of his vehicles.

Alexander's words went through her head again. And then she thought about her father, and how he had talked through his latest sermon on pride with her. He wanted to encourage their community not to be prideful in accepting the help that was offered to them after the fire.

Was she being prideful in not signing the agreement?

She looked at the dispersing crowd and her eyes were immediately drawn to Alexander, who was assisting one of the ladies to her car. He had a good heart, and she knew he'd meant well with the advice he'd given her. But he didn't know the whole story. He didn't know how Sam's father had taken advantage of her, then tossed her aside when he'd gotten what he wanted. He didn't know the lack of character, or how, despite the legal agreement, she didn't trust Bucky to keep his word. It felt like she'd be selling out her son for the sake of a temporary situation. Surely there was a way out.

But as she saw Mrs. Nelson, the librarian, getting into her car, Janie wondered if perhaps she was too optimistic. Mrs. Nelson was among those who had lost their homes, and furthermore, because the high school already had a librarian, she'd lost her job. So she was cutting her losses and leaving, moving to Denver to stay with her son until she could find a new job.

Many of the townspeople were doing the same.

It had been hard enough to make a living in the small ranching community. But with half the town gone and so many jobs lost, many people had no other options.

Janie had been happy to get her job as a teacher's aide at the elementary school. She'd originally gone to college to get a teaching degree, but had dropped out a semester shy of graduating to have Sam.

Her parents had worked so hard to send her to college, and she'd failed them.

As if he knew she'd been thinking about him, her father approached. "I'm so sorry about your job," he said.

Great. She was going to have to have this conversation with everyone who knew her.

"I'll be fine. I trust that God will provide, just as He always has," she said.

Her father nodded. "Ellen Adams is thinking about leaving town. Maybe you could talk to her about taking over her job at the community resource center."

"They're already low on funds. When Ellen told me they would be cutting my job, she admitted that she was also going to take a pay cut to keep the center running."

For a moment, her father looked thoughtful, then he said, "There are other grants, you know. I would imagine that with as hard hit as our town has been by the fire, our community is probably eligible for a lot of different grants. You should look into them."

She had done some work in that area, but not a lot. Still, if it could help their community, she might as well give it a try.

"I hadn't thought of that, but you're right. If you come across any resources, let me know."

Her father hugged her. "You don't always have to be strong. Are you taking the time you need to mourn your losses? Your mother, your home, the town?"

She hugged him back, then pulled away. "Are you? I'm doing what I need to get through."

"I am," he said. "Ricky has been a good friend to me, and we've spent a lot of time processing everything that's happened. But

I'm worried about you. Are you filling your well? Are you letting others in?"

Everyone asked her how she was doing, and she told them all the same thing—as well as can be expected.

Because that's what they were all doing. Once again, she thought about Alexander, and how he'd encouraged her to unburden herself on him.

"I'm trying," she said. "I've spent a lot of time with Alexander, and even though he encourages me to open up, it feels wrong because he's so closed off, and he has his own troubles to deal with."

Her father followed her gaze to where Alexander was standing. If you didn't know the community, you wouldn't know that he hadn't been part of their group forever, laughing and joking like they'd all grown up together. He fit in so well, but ever since he'd told her that he would be returning home at some point, it was hard to let herself get too attached.

"He seems like a good man," her father said. "You haven't dated anyone since moving back home, so I can see how you would be nervous. Still, you can't let your past pain dictate your future."

She watched as the kids ran from the playground to surround Alexander with hugs.

Sam tugged at his hand, then pointed in her direction. She smiled and waved at them, and Sam tugged at Alexander's hand again.

"Sam likes him," her father said.

"He's not staying," Janie said. "I don't know his timeline, but he's made it clear that he has a job and family in Denver."

Her father shrugged. "Denver is not that far away. A lot of people are leaving. It seems like every other family I've talked to has indicated that they don't have it in them to stick around and rebuild. There are better jobs elsewhere, and they won't have to go through the agonizing rebuilding process. Maybe it's time for you to spread your wings, too."

Janie stared at him. "But you just told me I should apply for grants for the community center and take that job."

"I'm just saying that you have options, that's all," he said. "Maybe it's time for you to look around at the open doors and see where they lead."

Before she could answer, Sam had let go of Alexander's hand and was running toward her.

"I have a child to think of."

Rather than waiting to hear what else her father had to say, Janie stepped forward to meet her son and gathered him up into a giant bear hug. He was getting big, almost too big to be picked up much longer. Before the fire, she'd noticed that his pant legs were a little too short. She'd wondered where she'd get the money to replace them, but she supposed one of the blessings of the fire was that they'd all be getting new clothes, and Sam could get some that fit.

"Guess what, Mom?"

"What?" Sam wriggled out of her grasp, so she set him down.

"Mr. Ricky said that those of us who wanted to could bunk down in the main house like a big campout. I could sleep with the men."

The way he said *men* made her want to giggle, but she knew he took his desire to be a man very seriously. That was the trouble with being a single mom. While Sam had several very good male role models, he often lamented the fact that he didn't have a dad.

"That sounds fun, but—" She didn't know how to break it to him that because she wasn't a man, she couldn't join them, which meant Sam couldn't, either.

"I asked Alexander if I could bunk down next to him, and he said yes if it's okay with you."

Sam turned to Alexander, but not before

Janie could see the way her son's eyes shone with hero worship.

This was why she hadn't dated since coming back home. She didn't want Sam getting his hopes up over every man who entered his life. As it was, he'd already asked several family friends to be his dad. The last thing she needed was for him to get an expectation of Alexander in that direction.

"All of the guys are doing it," Alexander said. "Kind of like a father-son thing, only Sam doesn't have a father and I don't have a son, but it seemed a shame for him to miss out."

Great. Exactly what Janie feared.

"Ty said I could be his son since Katie is a girl and no girls are allowed, but it would be more fun to have a pretend dad of my own."

It would be way more convenient for Sam to be with Ty, since Ty wasn't a single man for Sam to put hopes on about being his dad. Even though Katie had told Sam that she would share her new dad with him when Ty married Rachel, she heard the kids conspiring on multiple occasions about getting Sam his very own dad.

She looked from Sam to Alexander, then back at Sam again.

"I could go," her father offered. "Ricky put

me up in one of his guest bedrooms, thinking I would be more comfortable there, but it wouldn't be a hardship to sleep in the great room with my grandson for a night."

At least he understood her dilemma. Sam, however, looked angry at the suggestion.

"It's a father-son campout, not a poppa and his grandson." Sam kicked the ground. "Why can't I have a dad like all the other kids?"

Janie shot her father a look that she hoped expressed her gratitude for his attempt at stepping in.

Alexander squatted to Sam's height. "Your poppa is a great guy. Mine died when I was a little boy, so I didn't get to know him very well. Some people have dads, some have poppas, and others have really good friends who are willing to help out from time to time. You should be grateful for the wonderful men in your life. Not everyone has a poppa like yours, so if he's offering to spend time with you, then you should take it."

The solemn look Sam gave Alexander twisted Janie's heart in a funny way.

"But you asked me first," Sam said.

Alexander looked up at Janie's father. "How about you sleep between us?"

She knew Alexander was just trying to help, but she didn't think he realized how much this was setting her little boy up for heartbreak. She'd have to have a word with him later about making sure her son's heart didn't get broken when he left.

Sam looked over at her father. "Can we do that?"

Her father nodded. "Of course we can. I haven't had much of a chance to get to know Alexander, so this would be a great opportunity."

Alexander stood and ruffled Sam's hair. "See that? A win-win solution for us all."

Sam gave a fist pump. "Yes! And I can bring my dinosaur sleeping bag, and—"

Then he stopped. His face darkened. "It got burned up in the fire. I don't have a sleeping bag."

This was the hard truth they were all continually facing. Just when things started to feel normal again, they realized one more thing they had lost.

"We can get a new one," Janie said. "The insurance company gave us money to replace our belongings."

Sam shook his head. "No we can't. We got it at the hardware store, and the hardware store burned down too."

Another business that wouldn't be rebuilding. Steve Clark had already been mumbling about needing to retire for the past few years, but hadn't been able to find anyone to take over his business. Now he was taking the insurance money and his wife and moving to Arizona, where the winters were milder.

"We could take a drive to Buena Vista and see what they have," her father suggested. "I need a few supplies, and you could do with a few replacements to those borrowed clothes."

Then he turned to Janie. "We could all go. You haven't had a break, and like your son, you could do with some fresh new clothes that are all your own. It would be good for you to get away for a while."

Though Buena Vista wasn't a large town, it had a lot of the conveniences Columbine Springs lacked. It was also a lot closer than Denver. Still, it didn't seem right to leave when there was so much to do.

Alexander seemed to sense her hesitation. "Your father's right. You could use a break. And weren't you just telling me about the place there that has the best hamburgers in the world? You should go."

"Jerry's!" her father said. "I haven't had a Jerry Burger in years. Your mother was always on me to eat less red meat. We have to go."

The excitement in her father's voice made it impossible to refuse.

"I guess it wouldn't hurt to go. Rachel is low on groceries anyway, and while she says we aren't a burden, I'd love to save her the trip."

While Columbine Springs had a small convenience store that carried the basics, grocery wise, the nearest grocery store was either in Buena Vista or an hour in the other direction. Even though people were used to traveling to get groceries, it seemed like a much more difficult trip now, in the aftermath of the fire.

"You're coming, too, right?" Sam asked, tugging at Alexander's hand.

"I don't need anything," Alexander said. "This seems like a good opportunity for your family to spend some time together."

Janie's father stared at Alexander for a moment. "Aren't you wearing borrowed clothes as well? Yours were in the car at the church, and I understand the insurance company said that nothing was salvageable because of the smoke damage."

Alexander shrugged. "I got some when the Red Cross was handing things out. They're mine now."

The Red Cross had set up in the high school gym and were using it to pass out donated items. While a lot of it was just junk other people didn't want and thought the town could use, every once in a while someone came out with something useful. Janie and Sam were also wearing donated clothes, and it would be a relief for Janie to have something of her own. Alexander might not admit it, but deep down, he probably felt the same way.

"Then you should come," Janie said. "Especially if we're going to Jerry's. That burger alone is worth the trip."

Alexander hesitated, then nodded. "All right. Let me check in with Ricky and let him know my plans."

He glanced nervously at Janie's father, like a schoolboy afraid he was about to get grilled by his date's father. He probably was, but this wasn't a test to pass. If her father had issued the invitation, it meant Alexander had already passed, that her dad liked him and wanted to get to know him better.

And even though Janie was doing her best to shut off her heart to him, with her father and son so open to Alexander, it was becoming harder and harder to do.

Agreeing to go with Janie and her family to Buena Vista was a bad idea on so many levels. But Alexander hadn't known how to politely refuse, especially since it was at the pastor's invitation.

After making a few purchases at the hardware store and a discount store for some clothing basics, they'd walked to a quaint little park next to a gurgling creek so Sam could play and get out some of his excess energy. The sun had come out, and after such miserable gray days following the snow that had put out the fire, it felt good to relax in the warmer weather. Not warm enough to go without a coat, but the sun's rays still felt good on Alexander's face as he sat on one of the benches. Janie was running around with Sam, and it brought a smile to his face to see what an engaged mother she was.

He wished the senator could see what he saw. Had he even talked to Janie? Maybe they could have a conversation, and the senator would understand that Janie wasn't a threat.

Though Alexander had a vested interest in making sure Janie didn't talk, the more time he'd spent discussing Sam's father with her and her lack of information, the less he could see her going to the press. She was happy with her life, and she would surely know how disruptive it would be to be in the middle of a media circus.

It didn't explain the blackmail, but Alexander had to believe there was something they'd missed.

"I'm glad you decided to come with us today," the pastor said, sitting on the bench next to him.

Alexander looked over at him. "As much as I hate to admit it, you're probably right. I did need a break. It feels so good, sitting here in the sun and doing absolutely nothing. I've always seen ads for Buena Vista and places like the hot springs, but I've never had the time to visit. Now that I'm here, I wish I hadn't waited so long. I'll definitely be back." He grinned. "Especially to use the hot springs. With it so close to Columbine Springs, do you guys visit often?"

"No," the pastor said. "Like you, we're too busy. But sitting here, listening to the creek and my grandson's laughter, I'm reminded of the need to relax more. The hot springs are great, though. Buena Vista has two public ones. I hope you take the time to enjoy them while you're here."

When he'd seen the ranch website before coming, Alexander had all sorts of ideas of things he'd hoped to try. But the fire had intervened, and now he was just doing what had to be done.

"Maybe next time," Alexander said.

The pastor nodded like he understood. "When are you planning on leaving?"

It was a good question. Alexander wasn't sure he knew the answer to that himself. It all depended on whether or not the senator wanted him to stay. If the senator wanted him home, he had enough vacation to get him through Thanksgiving, but after that…

Sam's laughter rang out across the playground as he kicked a ball to Janie.

Then Sam turned to them. "Poppa! Alexander! Come play with us!"

For the first time, Alexander realized he didn't want to leave. Yes, his family was in Denver, but it wasn't that far of a drive, and he was so busy with work that he often didn't see them anyway. But that was the problem. Work. Even if Alexander chose to stay, it wasn't like there were a plethora of jobs for a political analyst in the middle of nowhere Colorado. Which meant his dreams of his own political career would be worthless.

"I'm not sure yet," Alexander said as he stood to join Sam and Janie. "I'll stay at least through Thanksgiving, but I do have a life I need to get back to."

Some life. He didn't want to tell the pastor this, but it wasn't much of one. Long days at the office often meant he'd go home, find something to eat, fall into bed, then do it all again the next day. Even on weekends, there seemed to be one event or another that he attended on behalf of the senator's campaign.

Alexander had always told himself that he was doing this for the benefit of the country. Because someday, he wanted to make a difference. But in all the things he had done, in all the political campaigns he'd worked for, he'd never felt more appreciated or valuable than he did being in Columbine Springs.

They kicked the ball around for a while, and even Janie's father joined them. For a short time, Alexander felt the weight of his troubles fall off of him.

After sending the ball past Alexander, Sam came running toward them, a wild grin on his face. "Mom says we can go eat now, and since I was a good boy, I get ice cream for dessert."

"Is the ice cream as good as the burgers?" Alexander asked, catching the little boy's excitement.

"Yes," Sam said. "It's not as good as our ice cream place, but it's still pretty yummy. I'm so glad it didn't burn down in the fire. This summer, I'll use my allowance and take you to buy one."

Alexander had seen the closed-up ice cream shop at the end of Main Street, and he'd been told it was only open in the summer. When he'd originally come to town, he thought it was a shame he'd never get to try it, but now he desperately wanted to do so.

And yet he wasn't sure how that was going to happen if Janie found out the truth about why he was in Columbine Springs.

"You don't need to spend your allowance on me," Alexander said, sitting on a nearby bench to tie his shoe before going after the stray ball.

"But I want to," Sam said. "I'm going to do so many chores for Poppa that I'll have enough money to get the big sundae."

How was he supposed to let the little boy down easily? He didn't need the nudge from Janie's father to know that the fact that Sam was willing to spend his hard-earned money on him meant a lot. Alexander wasn't stupid. How many times had Sam tugged on his hand and asked a question or pointed something out?

He meant something to Sam. And Sam meant something to him.

Which was why this whole situation was so messed up. They'd all been having fun, playing soccer like it was no big deal, but the simple action had brought them closer together.

"We'll see what happens," Alexander said,

trying to find a way to put some distance between them. "Remember, I live in Denver, so Columbine Springs is pretty far for me to come for ice cream."

Sam gave him a puzzled look. "But you live at Mr. Ricky's now. He is your poppa."

So much for the easy way out. He owed the little boy more than just a pat answer. Alexander tapped the open space on the bench next to him. "I'm staying at Mr. Ricky's. And yes, he's my poppa. But I have a job and a house in Denver. As much as I love it here, I can't stay forever."

He looked up to see that Janie had joined them, and she gave him a small nod, like she appreciated him not getting her son's hopes up.

"But how are you supposed to marry my mom and be my dad?" Sam asked.

Alexander closed his eyes briefly. He hadn't been prepared for this question. Nor the expectations of the little boy who just wanted someone to be his dad. He should've seen it coming, especially after the sleepover question.

"That's not in the plan, sorry, buddy," Alexander said, wishing he had a better answer.

Sam jumped off the bench and put his

hands on his hips, glaring at Alexander, then at Janie, then back at Alexander.

"I have been asking my mom for a dad for years. And every guy that I want to be my dad, Mom says that they don't have the special feelings that moms and dads have for each other. But Katie and Ryan heard their moms talking about how my mom looks at you like a tall drink of water."

A confused expression crossed Sam's face. "And that must mean that she has those special feelings for you. So why don't you have those feelings for her? My mom is the best mom in the whole world."

Alexander stared up at Janie, whose face was contorted into an expression that looked like she wasn't sure if she should be furious or burst out laughing, but knew that either response was going to upset her son.

And while it was flattering that Janie's friends thought Janie might be developing feelings for him, it only made Alexander feel even worse about the situation. It didn't feel like there was a way out. How could he break her heart? And yet, no matter what he did, it was inevitable. As soon as she found out the truth, it was over.

So he had to tell the best truth that he could, given the circumstances. "Your mom is the best mom in the whole world, after my mom."

It was weird, making that comparison to his mom, and realizing that as disappointed as he was in her for lying to him, she had still been a wonderful mother. One lie did not negate a lifetime of caring for him and his brother. At that moment, Alexander knew, beyond a shadow of a doubt, that he completely forgave her for her deception. She'd done everything to give Alexander and William the best life she could.

If he could forgive his mother, could Janie find a way to forgive him?

Alexander patted the spot Sam had vacated. "I know you want a dad, and if I were at a place in my life where I could have a son, I would want one just like you. But sometimes, things don't happen the way we want them to, and we have to learn how to be okay with that."

Then Alexander turned and looked at Janie's father. "Remember earlier, how I was telling you how you had a great poppa, and I didn't get to know mine? Be grateful for what you have, because when I look at all the men in your life who love you, I think a lot of little boys would love to be in your shoes."

The relief on Janie's face reassured Alexander. He was grateful that she was giving him a chance to handle this, and even more grateful that he was doing the right thing.

Sam hadn't moved from where he stood, but he did look up at Alexander. "Poppa tells me that a lot, too. Why do you think no one wants to be my dad, though? Mom won't tell me anything about my real dad, so he is either a really bad man, or he's a superhero. Who do you think he is?"

Sadly, Alexander knew exactly who he was. And Bucky was no superhero. But he couldn't tell this little boy who had so much confusion in his eyes what a worthless piece of garbage his biological father was. Even though Alexander had the utmost respect for the senator as a politician, even he would admit that the senator was a lousy father and an even worse poppa. As much as Alexander hated to admit it, Sam was lucky not to have them in his life.

The thought made him want to cry. He'd spent his whole career following the senator and his work, hoping to emulate him. And, yes, he believed in the senator's cause. But he wasn't sure he liked the man as a human being.

None of that was going to help the confused little boy standing before him.

Alexander held his arms out to Sam. "I can't tell you anything about your father, but I can tell you that you have a wonderful family who love and support you. And if they think that it's not good for you to know who he is, then you need to trust them."

Sam came into his arms, and Alexander hugged him tightly. "I'm sorry that I can't be who you want me to be. But like everyone else who loves you, I'll always be here for you."

Maybe it was the wrong promise to make to someone whose mother's heart he was about to break. But regardless of what would happen between Alexander and Janie, if Sam needed him, Alexander would keep his promise.

Judging by the expression on Janie's face, she didn't exactly appreciate it, but her father made an approving noise, like he understood Alexander did have Sam's best interests at heart.

"Do you have a business card?" Sam asked.

Alexander looked at him, trying to figure out where that came from. He did have business cards, but he'd made sure they were hidden away in his belongings.

"What do you need a business card for?"

Sam pulled away and looked at him with

a sincere, knowing expression. "Before Ty became Katie's dad, he made her the same promise. And then he gave her his business card so that she could call him whenever he needed him. Do I get a business card?"

Great. He'd inadvertently set up this little boy for thinking that he'd eventually become his father. Worse, giving Sam his business card would be the fastest way to give up Alexander's secret.

"I'm sorry, I don't. But when we get back to the ranch, if you get me a piece of paper, I'll write down my promise and my phone number so you'll always have it."

Wide-eyed, Sam looked at him. "You'll write down your whole promise?"

When the dust settled, no one would believe Alexander's word. But at least Sam would have it in writing that Alexander truly did care for him.

"My whole promise."

Sam grinned. "Good. Now let's go have ice cream."

Janie shook her head. "After you eat your burger."

Sam ran ahead to the car.

"I should get the ball," Alexander said.

He started toward it, and Janie followed. Or course she'd want to talk to him about what he'd said to Sam. But he stood by it. Sam needed to know that he wasn't the problem in this equation.

"I'm sorry if you felt I was overpromising. But I mean it. If Sam ever needs anything, he can always come to me. Even if it's twenty years from now."

Janie nodded slowly. "I get that. But Ty made that same promise to Katie, long before he married Rachel. You need to understand the hope that it's setting up in Sam's heart."

He hadn't known that, and maybe had he realized, he wouldn't have been so strong in his promises. Except that as he looked toward the car, where Sam was standing expectantly, motioning for them to hurry, he couldn't regret it.

Alexander picked up the ball and tossed it at Janie. "I'm trying. But I also can't let Sam think there's something wrong with him. He's a great kid."

Janie's father approached. "It's tough, living up to the boy's expectations. But you're doing just fine."

He glanced over at the other man, expecting a warning not to break anyone's heart. But there was none, only a warm smile.

"I hope you know I meant what I said. Even

if Janie and I were to have a falling-out, if Sam ever needs anything, you can call me, too."

To them, it probably was one of those vague, just-in-case kind of things. But the sinking feeling in Alexander's heart told him that was probably going to happen sooner rather than later, and the closer he got to that impending doom, the sicker Alexander felt.

No, not sick. Like he was suffocating, and the walls were closing in on him tighter and tighter.

Chapter Eight

The days after their trip to Buena Vista found them busier than ever. Janie had wanted to talk to Alexander about his conversation with Sam to make sure they were on the same page, but it felt like she'd barely seen him.

With the high school needing their gym back so they could accommodate the elementary school students, the Red Cross was vacating their outpost there. The community resource center occupied an old storefront on Main Street and had been left unscathed by the fire. The smoke damage was minimal, which made it easy to transfer all the donations the Red Cross had been sorting through at school to the resource center.

But without those extra volunteers, it left people like Janie working long hours trying to sort everything into piles—what they could use, what was junk and what could be donated elsewhere.

She picked up a box that seemed to consist mostly of pet supplies. People often didn't think about the animals displaced by disasters, so she was especially grateful for whoever had thought to send something for the pets. The question was, where would she put it?

Every available space was taken up with items for other needs. They'd sectioned off some of the conference rooms for people to meet with insurance adjusters or to talk to someone who could help them sort through their claims.

The large food pantry was overflowing with donated food, and people were still sorting items. They'd always had a place for those donations, since the resource center had always provided for the hungry in the community, but this was more than they'd ever received.

She paused at the door to Ellen's office. The door was ajar, and Ellen sat at her desk, staring into space.

Janie rapped on the door gently. "Do you have a moment?"

Ellen jumped, like she was startled, but then smiled. "Of course. How can I help?"

The question sounded fake, forced.

Janie set the box down on the floor, then sat in one of the chairs. "How about you start by telling me what's going on. You seem off."

Ellen sighed. "I'm sure your father has told you that I want to leave Columbine Springs. I know it sounds terrible, but I just can't stand looking at the rubble of the house Jim and I built together. And yet I feel guilty, leaving the community in the lurch."

She gestured at the overflowing stack of paper on her desk. "There are so many donations to process, and so many letters from people offering help, it's overwhelming. What I want to do is cry over the loss of everything I've held dear, but everyone is counting on me, so I can't."

Janie knew the feeling. But unlike Ellen, she wasn't eager to leave. "Let me help," Janie said. "I know most of the operations just as well as you. Let me do some of the work, and you can go back to wherever you're staying and have some time for yourself. Just the other day I went into Buena Vista with my father, and the time away was so refreshing."

Ellen shook her head. "I'd feel terrible asking you to do that. It's been weighing heavily on me that I had to let you go. But we're out of money, and I didn't have a choice. And here you are, helping anyway, and it makes me feel even worse."

"What else am I supposed to do? The community needs the help, paid or not. I got a severance package from the school, and since the house burned down, I don't have rent or utilities, and while I know I'll eventually need to find a new place to live and pay bills again, for now, money isn't the problem."

She felt a little like a liar saying that, considering all the expenses she would soon face weighing on her.

"You're going to have to find a place to live eventually. Where are you staying now?"

That seemed to be the most common thing people asked each other these days. "I'm staying with Rachel and Ty. Dad said that once things settle down, Sam and I can move back in with him if I want. He's staying at Ricky's so the Smiths can have his house until they decide what to do, but it sounds like they are thinking about moving to Texas to be closer to her family."

Ellen nodded. "Carol told me. I don't blame them. I don't blame anyone for wanting to leave. Which is why I'm glad you're here. How would you feel about taking over for me? With the budget cuts, the pay is probably less than what you were making at the school, but at least you'd be getting paid for something you're doing anyway. I can't think of a better person to take over my job than you."

Her father had mentioned this might be coming, but hearing it from Ellen made everything feel more permanent.

"I hate to keep you here if this isn't where you want to be," Janie said. "But are you sure I'm the right person for the job? I didn't finish college, so I don't have a degree."

Ellen smiled. "But you have a passion for the community, and the desire to do the right thing. You've done just about every job there is to do here. I'd be willing to consult with you over the phone if needed. Please tell me you'll think about it. I don't want to leave the community in the lurch, but I dread waking up every day and looking at the devastation around us."

"Of course," Janie said. "Do you have a job description or list of tasks I can go over so I can make sure I'm capable of doing them?"

Ellen reached into her desk and pulled out a folder. "Here. I put this together to give to the board so they could begin a job search if you weren't interested."

Janie took the folder and started to leave, then remembered the box she'd left on the floor. "Oh. I was going to ask you. We have some pet supply donations, but I'm not sure what to do with them."

"Talk to Sue. I think she was coordinating animal donations."

Janie nodded, then placed the folder on top of the box, which she carried out of the room. When she looked back at Ellen, Ellen had the same zoned-out look she'd had when Janie first came in. The fire had taken its toll on everyone in the community.

As she walked down the hall to see if she could find Sue, she ran into Alexander.

"Where are you going with that? Let me help you."

Before she could answer, Alexander had taken the box out of her arms and the folder slipped to the floor, its contents scattering all over the place.

"Oh," Alexander said. "I'm sorry. I didn't notice that there."

Janie smiled. "Don't worry about it. I can pick them up. Why don't you get the box to Sue, and let her know it's animal supplies. Hopefully she knows what to do with it."

As Alexander stepped over the papers, he paused, bending over one to read one. "Executive director of the community center? Is Ellen leaving?"

"Maybe," Janie said. "But please don't say

anything to anyone. I don't think she wants anyone to know yet. She's asked me if I want the job, but I'm not sure I can handle it. I asked for the job description and information so I can read through it to make sure."

The look he gave her boosted her heart. "Of course you can do it. You're a natural. No one in this community works harder than you, except maybe your father."

Janie shrugged. "Maybe. But there's a lot more to the job than just caring about people. I have to manage the finances, apply for grants and do all the administrative work. I've never done anything like that before."

As she spoke, it seemed like an even more daunting task. Over the years she'd applied for other jobs, but many of them had rejected her based on her lack of a college degree. Even though that wouldn't be the case with this job, she couldn't help worrying about whether or not it would be counted against them if she applied for grants.

"I have faith. You can do it. And if you want help with the grants, I'm your guy. I've done my share of grant writing in the past, and I'm pretty good at it. Let me know when you have some time, and I can go through the paperwork with you. It's not as bad as it looks."

She had to admit, she and Alexander

made a good team. With the help from her mom's bunco group, they had everything they needed for the town Thanksgiving celebration at Ricky's the following week. The menu had been planned, people were lined up to cook, the food was organized, and the dining hall, usually full of Ricky's guests, was being decorated and prepared for the town.

Working with Alexander had hardly seemed like work. And with his encouraging smile, she knew she would probably be able to easily navigate the paperwork for the job.

But what would happen when Alexander left?

"Sounds great," Janie said. "We're having dinner at the main ranch house tonight so I can spend some time with my dad, but I'm sure he won't mind if I sneak away for a bit to go over the paperwork with you. He's the one who encouraged me to do this in the first place."

"I look forward to it," Alexander said. The tone in his voice and the light in his eyes told her that he meant it.

As he walked off, carrying the box to find Sue, Janie couldn't help wishing once again that he was staying.

But at least he hadn't made promises he couldn't keep. Except for the one he'd made to Sam, but somehow, she had a feeling that if Sam ever chose to make good on the promise stated in the paper he carried around, Alexander wouldn't hesitate to keep it.

It was just frustrating that all the things she liked about Alexander were all the reasons she knew he wouldn't stay. He had commitments back home, and he was the kind of man to keep them, which she respected. But he said he'd be back, and maybe over time, they could…

What? It was crazy to even think about some sort of future with him. She'd once been that starry-eyed girl with dreams of forever. And look where that had gotten her.

She went to put her folder in her backpack, then returned to the main sorting area, where volunteers were processing donations. When she'd left earlier, Sam was there with Rachel and Katie, but now Sam was missing.

"Where's Sam?"

Rachel looked up from the box of clothes she was sorting. "Alexander stopped by to say hi, and Sam asked if he could go with him. Alexander said he didn't mind, so I let him. I hope that's okay."

"Of course it's okay," Katie said. "Alexander is going to be Sam's dad."

Not this again.

Janie closed her eyes and counted to ten before opening them and looking over at Katie.

"I'm sorry to disappoint you, but that's not going to happen. Alexander has to return to Denver to his job and family."

"We moved here from Denver," Katie said.

Janie looked over at Rachel, hoping her friend would bail her out.

"That's different," Rachel said. "I'm able to do my job no matter where I live. Alexander might not have that luxury."

Katie looked puzzled for a moment, then said, "Then he needs a new job. I'll ask Poppa Ricky, and he'll give Alexander a job."

It was always so simple for children. Even though Alexander had told her a little bit about his job, she still didn't know exactly what he did, or if he could find something here. And anyway, it was none of her business. If Alexander wanted to move to Columbine Springs, it had to be his decision. Not because a couple of kids had decided to make it so.

"You'll do no such thing, Katie Lynn. This is a grown-up matter and you need to stay out of it."

At least Janie and Rachel were on the same page. But sometimes, the way Rachel would ask Janie to help Alexander with something or vice versa, Janie had to wonder if Rachel wasn't trying to do a little matchmaking of her own. It seemed like everyone was pushing

Janie and Alexander together. On one hand, Janie didn't mind. But on the other, it was frustrating to have growing feelings for him when he'd already made it clear they didn't have a future.

"I'm going to go see where they got off to," Janie said. "If you see them before I do, tell them I'm looking for them."

She wandered through the center and finally spied Alexander and Sam sitting in a beanbag chair in a quiet corner in the back. Alexander had his arm around Sam, and he was reading her son a book. At first they didn't notice Janie, but when Alexander turned the page, he looked up and smiled.

"I hope you haven't been looking for us long," he said. "When I brought the box of animal supplies to Sue, she handed me a box of books that needed to go to another area, but the bottom broke open, and when I was picking them up I found one of my childhood favorites."

He held up the book and smiled. *Thomas the Tank Engine*, a series Janie knew well.

"It's one of Sam's favorites, too."

"I know," Alexander said. "He told me."

Then he put his finger to his lips and pointed down at Sam. He had fallen asleep in Alexander's arms.

"That's strange," Janie said. "He usually doesn't take naps."

Alexander gently brushed the hair off of Sam's forehead. "It's been a busy season for him. I'm sure if we could all take a nap, we would, too."

Janie nodded. "True. I hope he's not coming down with something."

Alexander felt Sam's forehead, then shook his head. "He hasn't acted sick, and he doesn't seem to have a temperature. I think he's probably just worn out."

Could her heart melt any more at the tender way Alexander cared for her son?

"You're probably right," Janie said. "But I feel bad that I haven't had the chance to spend time with him recently the way I usually do."

"Are you kidding?" Alexander asked. "He thinks he's having the world's greatest adventure. But even adventurers get tired. Don't beat yourself up. You're doing a great job."

He hesitated slightly, then said, "I don't mean to sound critical, but has his teacher said anything to you about his reading? I know he's only in first grade, but I was surprised at the words he struggled with. He seemed embarrassed about it, and I don't think he believed me when I told him he wasn't stupid.

I'm sure that's not how you raised him. Any idea what might be going on?"

Janie sighed. "He struggles with reading. His teacher says he's at the top of the bottom, which means he doesn't qualify for extra help."

"The top of the bottom? What does that even mean?" Alexander raised his voice slightly, and Sam shifted in his arms.

Janie put her finger to her lips.

"Right. Sorry." Alexander lowered his voice. "But that's a ridiculous thing to say about a child. What kind of crazy person would do that?"

"It's fine," Janie said. "I'm just trying to figure out a way to afford a reading specialist to help him."

It was the first time she'd admitted this to anyone, and doing so made her feel a little less alone.

"I'm sorry," Alexander said. "Maybe it's another reason to take the offer."

This again. It was easy for someone like Alexander to view it as a financial transaction. But he didn't understand everything Janie had gone through, all the reasons why it felt like blood money, and why she couldn't feel good about it.

But he also had another point. One he didn't press now, but one Janie kept thinking about. What if the money was God's answer to her prayers?

She'd always been afraid to talk to others about this because she feared the judgment she'd been under when she first came home, pregnant and unmarried. But maybe her father was right—that people weren't judging her for that anymore. That she was the only one judging herself. And maybe, if she talked to her trusted friends and sought their advice, they wouldn't judge her either.

Alexander hadn't, and it had been a relief to know that she wasn't as alone as she thought.

"I'll think about it," she said. "But it still doesn't feel right to me."

Alexander nodded. "Good. And if there's anything I can do, let me know, because I'm here for you both."

"For now. And then you return to your other life," Janie said.

She hadn't meant it unkindly, merely as a warning to him why she couldn't let herself get too close. But the hurt expression on his face told her he hadn't liked hearing it. She wouldn't take it back though. He had to understand why it was so important for her to protect her heart.

"I wish things could be different," he said quietly.

So he'd been saying, and while she wanted to believe him, she also wondered what was so permanent in his life that he couldn't change. While part of her felt it was unfair that she'd shared so much of her life with him and he didn't seem to be doing the same, she also knew that it wasn't fair of her to have that expectation when she hadn't told him everything, either.

"I'm going to get back to work," she said. "Let me know when Sam wakes up."

It was probably good that Sam was sleeping so they couldn't carry on this conversation. It felt like all they were doing right now was going in circles. Everyone wanted them to be together, but no one seemed to understand how they were both in such different places in their lives.

But as Alexander shifted Sam in his arms and her son snuggled closer to him, she couldn't help praying that whatever was keeping Alexander away would somehow change.

Alexander had never known the peace of having a child sleep in his arms the way Sam did. Once again, he marveled at how Bucky could have been stupid enough to turn down the love of a good woman like Janie, and turn his back on such a great kid.

He closed his eyes briefly, but the sound of two women talking forced him to open them once more.

"What do you mean there's no money for the Thanksgiving turkey?" one of the women asked.

"The store that usually donates them said they've already given so much free food to our town that they weren't going to give us turkeys."

He recognized the second voice as belonging to Shelley, who had been helping them plan the Thanksgiving festivities. She just told him yesterday that all the food was taken care of.

"What are you going to tell Janie? If we don't have turkey, we don't have Thanksgiving."

"I know," Shelley said. "I'm still figuring that out. If we could go around and get everyone to give us a couple of bucks, we could buy all the turkey we need, and Janie would never know."

Though he appreciated that the women were trying to spare Janie's feelings, he also knew that Janie would be disappointed they didn't tell her the truth. It was important to Janie that no one had to pay anything for this dinner. She had said it was tradition.

He shifted the sleeping boy out of his arms and onto the beanbag, then approached the women. "You can't lie to Janie. She'd be crushed. There's got to be a way we can get the turkeys without having to ask people in the town to give money."

The other woman shook her head. "I've called everyone I know. All the neighboring towns. Everyone feels that they've already given our town so much."

Alexander could understand where they were coming from. In the first few days after the fire, donations had poured in. But now they had slowed to a trickle.

"Let me see what I can do," he said. "I have some connections with some charities in Denver, and they might be inclined to help out a town that's lost so much."

As he spoke, he thought about the senator. He was always looking for a feel-good story where he could attach his name and show his compassionate side. Perhaps he could donate the turkeys, and when he came for the inevitable follow-up, he could see that Janie wasn't who he thought she was—and more importantly, he would see what a great kid Sam was. Granted, he didn't know how he would pull it off without Janie realizing his connection to the senator, but maybe if he could get the two of them in the same room together, they could find some common ground.

Shelley looked at him nervously. "I don't like the idea of misleading Janie. And I don't want to ask the town for the money. Are you sure you can get the turkeys?"

Alexander nodded. Even if the senator didn't go for his idea, Alexander had worked with several charities over the years so surely he could find someone to donate the turkeys.

"If I can't, I'll buy them myself."

Shelley's friend shook her head. "Oh, no. You don't have to do that."

Alexander shrugged. "My mom is the ultimate sale queen. If I tell her what we're looking for, I guarantee you she will find us the best, cheapest turkeys out there. It'll be fine."

Though Shelley's friend looked doubtful, Shelley nodded. "Are you going to invite your folks up for this dinner? We'd love to meet them. They should know how much their son has come to mean to this town."

Now that was something Alexander could not see happening, not in a million years. His brother would refuse to come, and he couldn't see his father wanting to go to a dinner at Ricky's. His mom would if Alexander asked, but she also wouldn't want to anger her husband and other son. It would be a nightmare for his family.

"I'm not sure they've come to terms enough

with the past to do so," Alexander said. "But thank you for thinking of them."

Shelley gave him a strange look. "You should at least ask them. Maybe they'll surprise you."

Even if they did come, one of his parents would surely make some boastful comment about how exciting it was that their son worked for the senator, and it would be all over.

That was the trouble with living his lie. There were so many things that could and would go wrong, and he wasn't sure how he would ever get out of the trap.

"I'll see what I can do," he said. "But other than the fact that there will be plenty of turkey for Thanksgiving, I make no promises."

The women seemed pleased by his answer, so they made their excuses and left. He turned back to where Sam was sleeping, and noticed the little boy was stirring.

Alexander gently sat next to him. "Did you have a good nap?"

Sam rubbed his eyes. "I don't take naps."

"I don't know what you call that, then." Alexander ruffled the little boy's hair and smiled. "We should go find your mom."

Sam got up, and as they wandered back through the center, Alexander realized that he knew every single one of the volunteers by name, and he knew parts of all their stories. Were he to remain in this town, he would call many of them friends. He'd worked in dozens of campaign offices, but he'd never had the kind of relationship with any of those volunteers that he did with these people.

Maybe he could change that when he got back to Denver.

They found Janie in the main office, coordinating schedules with one of the volunteers. She might not think she had the skills to run the place, but she didn't realize she was already doing so. He hoped that later tonight, as they went over the information about running the resource center, he could help Janie understand just how smart and capable she was.

As they were finishing up, the kids received an invitation to go with Rachel to a neighboring ranch where one of their friends lived, leaving Janie and Alexander alone.

"You ready to head back to the ranch?" Alexander asked.

Janie gave him a tired smile, and he wished he could do more to ease her burdens.

"That sounds good," she said. "On the way I have an errand to run, if you don't mind."

The woman never stopped serving others. One more thing Alexander couldn't reconcile with his mission. There didn't seem to be a selfish bone in Janie's body.

"What's the errand?" he asked.

"You'll see." This time, her smile filled her eyes, and he couldn't help thinking about how beautiful she was.

Though Alexander recognized the route they took as being somewhere on the Double R, he hadn't been to this part of the ranch before. He was struck by the vastness of everything his family had built. Funny how the thought of Ricky being family didn't stick in his throat the way it used to.

Janie pulled up in front of a gate leading to a pasture, but as far as Alexander could see, there was nothing around.

It hadn't yet gotten dark, but the sun was quickly fading behind the mountains and they didn't have much daylight left.

"What are we doing here?" he asked.

"You'll see."

She jumped out of the truck, then grabbed something out of the back before walking to the gate. Alexander followed.

Janie let out a long whistle, then four horses came running toward them.

Though most horses all looked the same to Alexander, he knew who these were.

"Lady!" he called out.

Janie reached into the bag and handed him a horse treat.

"The Petersons are staying with her sister in Denver until they can rebuild, and Connie is missing her horses. She wanted some pictures and updates. I thought it might be fun for you to visit the horses, too."

He'd never thought of himself as much of a horse guy, but seeing the horses he'd saved running toward him brought an unexpected joy to his heart.

Lady came right up to him, and when he offered her the treat, she nuzzled him like she remembered him.

"I think she knows you saved her life," Janie said softly.

Not this gratitude again.

"I'm not the hero you think I am," Alexander said.

Janie moved closer to him. "Maybe you're not who you think you are, either. We're the poorest judges of our own character."

She hesitated for a moment, then said, "You're a good man, Alexander, whether you want to admit it or not."

He turned to look at her. "I didn't say I was bad. But I'm also not the man you think I am."

Lady nudged him, like she wanted another treat.

"She's being disrespectful," Janie said. "Push her away when she does that."

Alexander gave Lady a small push, but she nudged him again.

"Harder," Janie said. "You have to show her who's boss."

"I don't want to hurt her."

Janie groaned. "You think a hundred-some-thing-pound man is going to hurt a thousand-pound horse with a little shove? You're too much of a softie."

No one had ever accused Alexander of being a softie before, at least not until coming here. He'd always managed to separate emotion from fact, priding himself on letting facts drive him.

Janie stepped between him and the horse, giving Lady a big shove when she tried to nudge Alexander again.

"Manners!" Janie said.

Lady whinnied at him, like she wanted Alexander to step in on her behalf. Funny, it was just like when he was growing up. He and William had known that if Mom said no, they could always ask Dad. This seemed to be what Lady was doing here.

Alexander held out his hands. "I don't know anything about horses, Lady. So if Janie says so, you've got to do what she says."

Crazy how naturally it came to talk to the horse like she was a person.

The other horses crowded around, but Alexander didn't know them like he knew Lady.

Still, they acted like they remembered him and how he'd saved Lady.

"Should I give them a treat, too?" he asked.

"Only if they mind their manners," Janie said. "Watch."

She reached into the bag and got out a treat. But before offering it to the horse closest to him, she said, "Stand."

The horse was obviously standing, so it seemed funny to Alexander for her tell it to do so. But something in the horse's demeanor calmed, then Janie offered it a treat.

"Now you do it," she said.

He took the treat and held it out. "Stand," he said.

Janie snatched it out of his hand before the horse could. "No. Be firm. And wait for the horse to give you its attention. Then offer it the treat."

This time, when he tried again, he did as Janie said, and he was surprised at the difference in the horse's demeanor.

"Better," Janie said. "See how much easier it is when you make them mind their manners?"

The encouragement in her voice brought a

lightness to his heart. Janie was such a good woman, capable of so much. She would do an amazing job running the community center. She'd been so patient with him here, and he'd seen her heart for others the entire time he'd been in Columbine Springs.

Janie handed him treats for the other horses, and as he gave them each a treat, he felt a peace in his heart he hadn't known before. Strange, considering everything in his world seemed to be so unsettled. He still had so much to accomplish, including the mission with Janie.

Watching Janie pet one of the horses and whisper things to it, he didn't feel the same level of dread he often felt around her. The piece of his heart that wanted to like her, to know her on a deeper level, didn't seem to be as afraid.

He'd offered some prayers, not knowing if they did a bit of good, but maybe hoping they'd do something. Could they be the explanation for the peace he felt?

Alexander turned to Janie. "I was wondering about the stuff you told me about God."

She gave the horse another pat. "You know I'm always happy to talk about God. What's on your mind?"

The gentleness in her voice made him feel

safe. But in the same moment, it also made him hate the way she'd told him what a good man he was. Did a good man plot to hurt a good woman, then ask her for ways to get God on his side?

No, this wasn't about getting God on his side.

But he did long for that peace Janie once talked about.

"I've been praying. I don't know why. I guess it feels like the right thing to do. But since I don't know that I really believe in all this stuff, do you think God is listening anyway?"

Janie came over and gave his arm a gentle squeeze. "I know He is. Prayer is really just about talking to Him and sharing your heart with Him. I think it's good that you're asking questions and choosing to pray anyway. God hears you."

But Alexander knew that just because God heard you didn't mean God was going to give you the answer you wanted. After all, despite people's prayers, the town had been ravaged by fire. Yet part of it was spared.

So what did that mean for all the prayers Alexander had made on Janie's behalf? Was there a way out of this mess?

Chapter Nine

The more time that had passed since the fire, the fewer people were camped out in Ricky's great room. Tonight, as Janie entered the house, she realized there weren't any more cots and sleeping bags piled up in the room. It had been returned to its former glory, and she wondered whether that meant more people had found places to stay, or more had given up.

As she crossed the foyer, Sam took off running up the stairs to the guest suite where his grandfather was staying. Alexander stepped out of the study.

"Where did everyone go?" she asked.

"A couple families said their houses are now habitable enough to go back to, and others were going to go spend Thanksgiving with family out of town. We were able to rearrange things so that no one is sleeping on the floor anymore. I've got the couch in the den."

Only someone who had been spending over a week sleeping on the floor would be excited about sleeping on the couch. This was not something he could have planned on, and yet, he'd taken it all in stride.

"Hopefully, with everyone gone now, you'll get to spend more time getting to know Ricky and Rachel," Janie said. "I feel bad that you spent most of your time with me, when you could've been working on projects with them."

He gave her a smile that made her tingle all the way down to her toes. "Don't be. I enjoy our time together. I'm just glad you still choose to spend time with me, even though I can't be who you want me to be."

The sadness in his voice whenever he said that made her heart hurt for him. She wanted to tell him that it didn't have to be that way, that he could open up and trust her, but it would mean she would have to do the same for him. And she wasn't sure she was ready to risk her heart like that.

Still, it felt like something had changed between them earlier, when they'd visited the horses. Alexander's heart was changing, even if he wasn't ready to admit it yet.

"I don't need you to be anyone but yourself," she said. "And I like spending time with you, too."

He gestured at a nearby sofa. "Did you bring the paperwork about the director position? Sam will probably be up with your dad for a while. We should have time to go over it."

She should be getting the message by now. Every time she tried to talk to him about something personal, he always changed the subject. On one hand, she appreciated that he was trying to guard her heart. But on the other, it only made her more curious.

What did he think he was protecting her from?

She'd already put herself out there, multiple times, and he kept closing the door. She'd learned from the past that forcing a relationship where it wasn't wanted was destructive. Everyone had told her that Sam's father was a player, and that leopards didn't change their spots. But he told her she was beautiful, made her feel special, and she'd bought all his lies. However, after he'd gotten the one thing he wanted from her, his tune changed, and she had to chase him.

She wasn't going to chase Alexander.

When they started going over the paperwork, the romantic thoughts quickly disappeared as Alexander began explaining what a lot of it meant. Though he said many of the things listed were what she was already doing, it sounded like a lot more. Overwhelmingly so.

She'd seen the stack of paperwork on Ellen's desk, and it would take her hours to get through it. Even Ellen had admitted that the paperwork alone often kept her from interacting with their clients, which was what Janie loved the most about her job.

Though she knew she should be paying attention to what Alexander said, her mind drifted to the question of whether or not she was willing to trade the parts of the job she loved for a paperwork nightmare that would be paying her less than what she'd barely been getting by on.

"As for the grants," Alexander was saying, "I don't mean to knock Ellen, but she didn't do a very good job of researching the programs out there. I did a quick internet search of a few ideas that I had, and at least fifty different grant programs popped up. I see the potential in what the resource center can do, and there isn't any reason why you couldn't get the grant money to fund an executive director position, like the one you're considering, at a higher rate, as well as staff to help."

He stood. "I could get my laptop out of the other room and show you."

He'd done all that work already?

"You put a lot of thought into this. Why do you care so much, when you've already told me that you're leaving?"

Alexander shrugged. "Just because I can't stay doesn't mean I don't care. I came here not knowing what to expect, and I met a community of generous, loving people who accepted me with open arms."

He gestured at the door to the study. "I have more hand-knitted scarves and blankets than I could use in a lifetime. I'll keep them, because I know the ladies went to a lot of trouble to make them for me as a thank-you for what I did to help them. I have enough promises of home-cooked meals once people get settled that I could probably go a year without cooking for myself."

That sounded a lot like the town Janie knew and loved. "But remember, you did a lot for them, too. That's what being in a small town is about. You probably don't get a sense of that in a big city like Denver, but I hope you know that the love you feel here is genuine."

Alexander looked thoughtful for a moment,

then he nodded. "I do. But that's not why I did any of this. I saw a need, so I jumped in to help. I know people keep saying it's not what anyone would do, but that's how I was raised. My mom and dad would be furious with me if I turned my back on people needing my help. And I would feel bad about it, too. I've been given so many privileges and gifts others don't have. It's only right that I share what I have."

Then he gave a quick shake of his head. "Anyway, I'll grab my laptop and show you what I found."

When he left the room, it gave Janie the chance to think about what a good man Alexander truly was. And maybe what she liked most about him was that he didn't put on airs or think he was someone special. When she dated Bucky, he'd made a big show of taking her to a local homeless shelter to serve a meal. He'd been so puffed up about how he volunteered and gave back to the community, but it had all been an act. He'd done it for the recognition and admiration of others, and looking back, Janie should have seen that as a warning sign about the state of Bucky's heart.

Alexander was different.

It made her all the more certain that he was someone worth pursuing. So how did she pursue him in a way that didn't scare him off or make her seem desperate? That, and she still had to figure out the distance issue. She supposed she could take it slow and let things happen naturally. Even living in Denver, he'd visit his family sometime. Maybe he'd find a reason to stay. She sent a quick prayer to God about allowing Him to pave the way and letting Him guide her steps and decisions with Alexander.

When he returned to the room, she felt better about their relationship.

He pointed at the screen, where he showed the search results for various grants. "This one would be perfect for you guys. It's not very big, but I've met the director of the foundation at several events, and she's great about connecting other people. If you applied for this grant and got it, you'd be invited to their annual luncheon, in which you would be able to network with other people and organizations that serve their communities. I didn't want to be presumptuous, but I'd be happy to print out this list for you so you can take a look and see for yourself."

He spoke with such confidence that while Janie knew he intended to make her feel better about taking on this project, it only made her feel worse. She didn't have the same confidence and skills that Alexander did. He would be amazing at this job.

"You should apply, not me," she blurted.

Alexander shook his head. "I already have a job. Even with additional grant money, this wouldn't pay nearly what I make. Besides, I have full confidence that with a little nudging in the right direction, you could do this. You could make the community resource center even better than it was before."

He was way more optimistic than she was. He scrolled down the page. "And here. You were saying that Sam didn't qualify for any extra help from the school with his reading, but this grant is a program that gives additional money to small communities to help boost literacy in elementary-school children. So you could get the grant for the community, and help not just Sam, but other students who might be in his position."

The passion in his voice made her wish he was staying. He might say he had another job that he loved. But whenever she asked him about that job, he sounded nervous, afraid. While she understood that he had to comply with his nondisclosure agreement, it didn't sound like his job gave him the kind of satisfaction he was getting helping the community here.

Plus, he'd spent the little free time he had researching grants for the center as well as one specifically to help Sam. Alexander might not realize it yet, but he belonged here.

Janie looked at the qualifications for the grant Alexander pointed out. It would help a lot of people. And it felt good to look at a solution for everyone, not just her. Could she make it work?

As Alexander continued explaining the grant, she leaned in more toward him. She couldn't help also noticing his clean and refreshing scent. He shifted his weight and put his arm around her, allowing her to get closer to the computer. It was almost like being snuggled up to him. And it had been so long since she'd been in a man's arms.

She could get used to this.

She didn't know how long they'd been working when Sam came running back into the room. "Mom! Alexander!"

They both jumped, bumping each other, and for a moment their eyes locked. Had Sam not been right there, Janie wondered if Alexander might have kissed her.

But that was silly. She turned away and smiled at her son. "What's up?"

"Poppa said that Katie is going to eat with

us, too, and I wanted to go to her house to get her. But he said I had to ask you first."

Janie smiled at her son. "Is he going with you? I don't want you walking the ranch by yourself."

He looked over his shoulder. "Are you?"

Her father laughed. "Of course I am. I wouldn't let you go on your own." Then he looked over to Janie and Alexander. "Are you two getting a lot of work done?"

Janie nodded. "I didn't realize there was so much funding available out there for some of the things Ellen and I have wanted to do but didn't have the funds for. There are grants specifically to help with them. I feel like a whole new world is being opened up for the community."

She looked over at Alexander. "He's a whiz at all of this. I wish he could stay longer to help me get it all off the ground."

Alexander scooted away. "I wish it were possible. But like I told you, I'm always just a phone call away. Anything you need, I'll do my best to help you."

It didn't seem like much, but it would have to be enough. No, that wasn't giving him due credit. Someone who was as knowledgeable and talented as Alexander didn't offer their expertise for free. He'd even admitted that his current job paid way more than anything he could get working for the resource center. He was giving them a gift. One of many he'd already given, and he was probably too humble to accept any praise.

"Thank you," she said. "I'm still not sure I can do this, but you seem to think I can, and you offered to help so I'm going to give it my best shot."

"I believe in you, too," her father said. "You don't have to do this alone. We're all here to help, if you let us."

From the way he talked, she suspected that was what he had been trying to tell her all along. She would admit that before the fire, she wouldn't have been so willing to receive all the help she'd been given lately. Maybe she had been too stubborn, trying to handle everything alone.

As much as she wanted Alexander to stay, she'd also been pushing him away with her insistence on keeping her secrets. They'd both been using her secrets as a way to keep each other at arm's length, and even though Janie said that she needed to know Alexander's secrets before sharing hers, maybe she should be the brave one and go first. Her shame had controlled her, and if she was going to be free of the past, she needed to come clean with it all.

Tonight, after dinner, she was going to tell Alexander everything.

It had been a long time since Alexander had gotten such a rush off working on a project. He'd done all sorts of grant proposals over the years, worked on creating bills for the legislature, but being a part of the community in which the work would be making such a big difference was something special.

Sure, he'd gotten letters from grateful constituents. But he'd also seen the hateful ones from people who didn't agree with policies. He'd even met some of them in person at various town hall events. But he didn't know any of them, not like this.

He sat back in his chair after finishing the meal, watching Rachel and Janie laugh at the kids' antics. He'd always wondered what it would be like, his family growing to a point where the next generation sat at the dinner table. He hadn't gotten to a place where he felt comfortable settling down, and William had his share of failed relationships, but being part of this family scene made Alexander wistful.

There'd been a spark today between him

and Janie, and the expression in her eyes at the time had told him that she felt it, too. If he were honest with himself, he would say that what he wanted most in the world right now was to follow that spark and see where it led. It had killed him when Sam had asked him to be his father. Bucky didn't deserve a kid like Sam. And Alexander would do anything for the little boy. He wanted to call out Bucky for being such a self-absorbed jerk.

The senator was wrong for wanting to hide Janie and Sam. They would be an asset to his campaign. People would like the senator more for owning up to his son's irresponsible actions. They'd respect him for stepping up and doing the right thing.

But it didn't explain the blackmail.

As he looked over at Janie, he still couldn't make sense of that. As angry and prideful as she was over the situation, there was no way she could be taking the senator's money.

But he'd examined and reexamined the letters.

"Let's play hangman," Katie said.

It must have been a popular game in the family because Janie got up and walked over to a drawer, from which she pulled out a notebook that she plopped down in front of everyone.

As Janie drew out the details of the game

and each kid called out different letters, Alexander stared at them, trying to see if they matched up to any of the writing in the blackmail letters. He'd already tried observing her handwriting as they dealt with fire-related issues, but it didn't seem to match.

Could someone else have written the letters for her?

Janie passed the notebook over to Rachel, and Alexander tried to look at her writing as well. But there were no similarities.

What did it all mean?

Even though the senator would probably accuse him of having ulterior motives, the right step would be to ask him if there was another angle. Another explanation for the blackmail. There was no sign of the money, no indication of Janie's willingness to take the money, and the handwriting didn't match. Alexander wasn't skilled at blackmail operations, but nothing about the situation could convince him that Janie was blackmailing the senator.

But could he convince the senator of that?

"I don't like this game," Sam said. "Let's go play a better one."

Alexander's heart ached for the little boy who was frustrated at playing a game with letters. It wasn't Sam's fault that he couldn't read the same way everyone else could. But, hopefully, Janie would pursue the grant and get Sam the help he needed.

"Poppa Ricky has Candyland," Katie said, jumping up from her seat and running out of the room. Sam followed, and Alexander couldn't help but smile at how the two of them got along.

"They're something else," Alexander said.

Rachel nodded. "You're telling me. You should see them when Ryan gets in the mix. The three of them are going to take over the world someday."

Everyone at the table laughed, and once again, Alexander felt full of the love of family. It was just like being at home, only his parents and brother were missing. Maybe he would see if he could talk them into coming for Thanksgiving. William needed to know these people, and understand the love from them. And even though his parents weren't technically related, by the way Ricky included Janie and her family in the mix, he knew they would feel the same warm welcome.

He just wished he'd taken the time to learn more about his family heritage a long time ago.

But maybe it wasn't too late.

"I know we're doing the town Thanksgiving," Alexander said. "But I came here hoping to learn more about my heritage. My mother's family brings a lot of traditions from their Scandinavian roots, and I know we have Mexican roots. What traditions do we have?"

Ricky shrugged. "Thanksgiving is an American holiday. We do what the Americans do. Have turkey, lots of food and family time. We just like any excuse to get together and celebrate. Besides, we are Americans. I'm the fourth generation on this land, and you're the sixth. We are proud of the life we built here, and of having such a successful ranch."

Then Ricky stood. "But we do honor our Mexican roots, and we honor the ancestors who came before us. I'm sure you've seen the pictures around the house of our history, but let me take you for a more detailed tour. I'm sorry I haven't gotten the chance to explain it to you sooner."

When Alexander stood, Rachel did the same. "I'd like to join you as well. I've heard the stories, but it seems like every time you tell one, there's a new detail, and I love hearing about my family." She looked over at Alexander. "If it's okay with you, that is."

He nodded. "I'd like that. I'm still getting used to the idea of finally having family who look like me, instead of being the oddball in a group of light-haired, light-skinned, blue-eyed Norsemen. What does your family think of you exploring your roots?"

His question appeared to hit a nerve in Rachel, whose face darkened.

"My mom died when I was ten, and I never knew my father. So I grew up in foster care. Coming here gave me the family I never had."

He hadn't thought about Rachel's past until now. And while they had worked together somewhat during the fire, he hadn't gotten to know her personally. But from what he did know, he liked her.

One more reason to talk to the senator and figure out a way out of this mess.

Not only did he not want to lose Janie, but he wasn't sure he could lose his sister as well.

As Ricky took them on a tour through the ranch house, he explained how this had been the original home of the first Ricardo Ruiz when he came to America, and how and where it had been added on to over the years. This wasn't just a house, but a place of living history.

Every photo on the wall, every piece of artwork and even much of the furniture spoke of the history of this ranching family who'd settled in a wild land and created a life for themselves.

Alexander found himself pausing at the large photo of his father, Cinco. He saw it every day, but for the first time he really looked at the man he'd refused to accept as being his father because it had felt like a betrayal to the man who loved him and cared for him his whole life.

The expression on Cinco's face was so much like William's when he was annoyed. He could almost picture Cinco telling the photographer to hurry up and take the picture because he had better things to do, just like William would.

When Ricky took them back to his office, he closed the door behind them.

"It might look fancied up now, but this room was the original cabin my great-grandfather built. If you move the bookcases, you can see some of the original log chinking. I wish my predecessors had done a better job of preserving it, but I think the wives got involved and thought it was ugly, so they covered it up." He moved a set of books to reveal a small safe.

"I put the ranch in a trust to preserve it, so there isn't much for me to leave for you. But I do have a few things that mean a lot to me, and I want to share them with you while I'm alive so you can hear the stories and appreciate them."

Alexander's throat closed with tears. He hadn't been expecting this.

Ricky pulled a small, hand-carved wooden box out of the safe and opened it. He held it out to them. "My great-grandfather loved to carve. When he was on the long cattle drives, he would sit by the fire, carving things. Then he'd give them to his wife when he returned. My grandmother threw most of them away because she thought they were junk. But this box survived, and it is our greatest family treasure."

Then he opened the box and emptied its contents. Four coins.

"Most people don't know this, but they had four sons. The first one was my grandfather, and the others died tragically as young adults. But when my great-grandfather came home with the proceeds from his first big sale, he set aside these four coins for his four boys. He had big dreams for the ranch, and he always wanted the boys to remember its humble beginnings."

Ricky gave each of them a coin. "I'm told they're worth a great deal, but to me they're priceless. You can sell them if you want, but I hope you'll keep them as a reminder of where you came from."

He looked over at Rachel. "I'd intended to give you one as a wedding gift, but I got distracted, and then there didn't seem to be the right time. But it feels right for me to share with you now."

Alexander was crying like a little boy, and when he looked over at Rachel, she was openly sobbing as well. Alexander reached forward and hugged Ricky, but Ricky brushed him off.

"I'm an old man, and I won't be here forever." He pointed at Rachel. "But she is your sister, and while I know you two don't know each other well, I hope in time, you can learn to be there for each other. Rachel has the finest husband a woman could ask for, but nothing beats the love of family."

Alexander turned and held his arms out to her. She stepped into his hug, and he held her tight.

His baby sister. He had William, but who did she have?

An amazing family, that's what. And it killed him to think that if he didn't find a way to fix things, he might be the one to destroy them all.

"I'll always be here for you," Rachel said.

That was supposed to be his line, but it felt good to have someone say it to him.

They talked a few minutes more, then Ricky said, "All right now, enough of this mushy stuff. You two play with the young ones, and I'm going to relax for a bit."

Rachel gave Alexander one last hug as they stepped out of the room. "I know we keep pushing you toward Janie. But I want you to know, it's only because we love you both. And if things don't work out, that's okay."

He nodded, then gave her another quick hug. "Thanks. That means a lot. I'm not ready for a relationship, and I'm doing my best not to make any promises I can't keep. I wouldn't hurt her for anything in the world."

"I know," Rachel said. "You're a good man. I wouldn't want you with her if I believed otherwise."

Her praise only made him feel worse. He'd been planning to wait to call the senator, but with everything so heavy on his heart, he had to do it now.

"You go on ahead with the others. I have a call to make, and then I'll join you."

He went into the den and closed the door behind him, then pulled out his phone. The senator answered on the first ring.

"Well? Is it done?"

Alexander took a deep breath. "No. I think we're barking up the wrong tree. I don't think Janie is blackmailing you. Is it possible that someone is making it look like it's Janie to cover their tracks? I see no evidence of your money being spent by her. Every time I've pressured her to take the money, she staunchly refuses, almost to the point of being offended. I looked at her handwriting, and it doesn't match the blackmail letters. We've got to be missing something."

"I am not paying you to investigate her. I'm paying you to get her signature."

Alexander was glad they were doing this over the phone, and not in person. Because he wasn't sure how he would keep from losing his temper.

"But if it's not Janie, her signature isn't going to get the blackmail to stop. You need to dig deeper."

The senator's loud sigh told Alexander that he might have gotten through to him. "I'll get an investigator on it. But I still need that signature. Who knows who will get to her?"

If anything, the senator's paranoia convinced Alexander all the more of his need to be in touch with people and get to know them personally. If the senator had only done that with Janie, he would understand.

"I've spent a lot of time with her, and used every angle I could to pry Bucky's name out of her. She still refuses to name him. She's not a threat."

He half expected the senator to argue, but when he remained silent, Alexander continued. "And that's what else I wanted to talk to you about. As you know, their community has been hard hit by a wildfire. They're planning a Thanksgiving celebration, but everyone who usually donates turkeys to them has donated other supplies, so they can't do the turkeys this year. I thought if you could donate the turkeys, it would be an excellent photo opportunity. It could boost your campaign."

While he had the senator's attention, Alexander took a deep breath and said, "It would also give you the chance to meet Janie and see for yourself what kind of woman she is. And it wouldn't hurt for you to meet your grandson. Sam is a great kid, and rather than being a liability, I think they could be assets to you."

"You're doing a lot of thinking for someone who's not paid to think. I gave you orders, and it sounds like you're doing everything but following them."

He should've expected this. After all, he was a lower-level employee, without the experience of some of the senator's senior advisors. But it was a good idea, and he would have been wrong to keep it from the senator.

"You don't have a lot of support in the smaller communities of our state. Giving them their turkey and celebrating Thanksgiving with them would go a long way to improving your image."

"I don't need to improve my image!" the senator practically yelled. "If you'd been in the office, you'd see my latest polling numbers. I'm going to win, easily, and I need to make sure that little tramp and her brat don't ruin it for me."

"She's not a tramp," Alexander said, unable to keep his voice steady. "Janie Roberts is a good woman with a loving heart, and no one who knows her would describe her that way."

He hoped the silence on the other end was a good sign, but the sinking feeling in Alexander's stomach said otherwise.

"That good woman sent another blackmail note, saying that with the fire her circumstances have changed, and she's going to need double the amount of money outlined in the nondisclosure agreement to keep her mouth shut."

There was no way. It couldn't have been Janie.

"There has to be a mistake. I specifically talked to Janie about the change in her circumstances, and suggested that taking the money you offered could be a solution. She was very much against the idea. Why would she tell me one thing, then send a letter to you, saying something completely different? That doesn't make sense."

The senator made an annoyed noise. "Whether it makes sense or not, that's what she did. I'm texting you a picture of the note so you can see for yourself."

The phone beeped with the text, and while the note looked like all the others in his file, it still didn't look like anything from Janie.

"This still doesn't mean it's her. You need to get an investigator to find out who's really behind this."

Finally, the senator said, "Let me make myself clear. Your only job is to get that woman's signature on the nondisclosure agreement. If you are not back in the office at the end of the Thanksgiving holiday with that signature, consider your employment terminated, and I will find someone more qualified to do the job, no matter what it takes."

He hung up before Alexander could respond, leaving Alexander to stare at his phone, wondering what had just happened.

Thanksgiving. He had until Thanksgiving to get Janie's signature.

While it would be disappointing to lose his job, Alexander had plenty of contacts elsewhere in the political community, and he could find something. It would just delay his timeline a little. But more worrisome than that was the threat about Janie.

The senator had tried an investigator. He'd tried the gentle touch with Alexander. So what would he do to coerce a woman to sign a document that she didn't want to sign?

Alexander took a deep breath, then noticed the door was slightly ajar. He was sure he'd closed it behind him. When he went to the door, he opened it and saw Janie standing there. She pushed her way into the room.

"What on earth did I just overhear?" she asked.

Chapter Ten

❧

She couldn't have heard what she'd just heard. There had to be a rational explanation. But from the look on Alexander's face, it was exactly what she'd thought.

"Who was on the other end of the phone?" she asked.

The guilty look on his face gave her the answer before he spoke. "That was Senator James Blackwell. He's my boss. He claims you're blackmailing him to remain silent over Sam's paternity."

Now that was something she hadn't expected. Yes, she had thought he was talking to the senator. But she hadn't considered how deeply involved Alexander might be.

"But I told him it had to be a mistake," Alexander added quickly. Too quickly. Like he felt guilty.

"That's why you kept encouraging me to sign the papers and take the money?"

She didn't know why she was even bothering to ask. The answer was obvious. But she could feel herself shaking, and somehow had to find a way to get her emotions under control.

"Yes," Alexander said. "He's running for the US Senate, and he's afraid that if people find out about Sam, it will hurt his chances of election. All he wants is for you to remain quiet, and the blackmail to stop."

That was the second time he'd mentioned blackmail.

"But I'm not blackmailing him," she said.

He ran his fingers through his hair and plopped down on the couch. "I know. That's what I've been trying to tell him. He's desperate for your signature, and I don't know how to convince him that someone else is behind this."

She almost believed him. But, of course, she would, because this whole time, she had believed in his sincerity about Sam deserving support. About wanting to help her.

"So everything you told me was a lie," she said.

He looked up at her, and if she didn't know

he was a first-class actor, she'd almost believe the forlorn expression on his face.

"I never lied to you. Yes, I deliberately withheld the truth from you on some things, but I always avoided lying. Everything I told you was the truth."

Wow. He was an even better manipulator than Bucky, and that was saying something.

"News flash. Deliberately misleading someone is still a lie."

The pathetic look on his face remained as he said, "The only things I misled you on were who I worked for and the fact that I already knew who Sam's father was. Everything else was the absolute truth."

Did he even know the meaning of the word? Probably not, working for the senator, who definitely did not. To him, the truth was whatever he wanted it to be at the time. As a loyal employee of the senator, Alexander would be no different.

How could she have been so fooled by him? She'd worked so hard to protect her heart, and somehow, Alexander had found a way to slither in and get her where she was most vulnerable. The Bible said that wolves often came disguised in sheep's clothing, and until now, she had no idea how true it was.

Alexander stood, then looked at her. "I

know I have a lot to make up for. But I'm on your side. Like I said, I don't believe you're blackmailing him."

He pulled out his phone and scrolled, then showed her a picture of a blackmail note. "Any idea who could have written this?"

She glanced at it briefly, then shook her head. "No. And I don't know who would pretend to be me. I've told you a thousand times. I have not told anyone about the situation. You were the first person I trusted enough to tell, and look where it got me."

That was the kicker. All the things she thought the Lord was doing in her heart, all the ways she was trying to open up. And for what? To be lied to again?

"I'm sorry," Alexander said. "I didn't know you when I first came here. I was under the impression that you were a lying blackmailer. But as I got to know you, I quickly realized it was wrong. I knew there had to be a misunderstanding, and I've been trying to talk to you, to find ways to make the information I had about you make sense."

Just like Bucky. Always trying to justify himself and his lies. "And you couldn't have said something like, 'hey, I heard you were blackmailing the senator, do you think you can tell me your side of the story'?"

She probably sounded a little hysterical, but she felt that way. She'd hated it when that investigator came to see her, but at least he was honest. He told her exactly what he wanted, and he left when she told him no. But that didn't seem to be how Alexander operated.

"After hearing your pain at the mention of Sam's father, I didn't think you'd be open with me."

Did he actually hear his own words?

"Of course I wasn't going to be open with you. You worked for the senator. And so you think manipulating me was the better option? You have some nerve."

"Does it matter to you at all that I think you're innocent?" he asked. "I've been trying to understand how anyone could think you guilty. Or who would be posing as you, because they have to know enough about you and the situation to be blackmailing the senator. Whoever it is knows exactly how much money you were offered. You're sure you haven't told anyone?"

Did he honestly think she was dumb enough to believe that he was trying to help her? No, he was probably just trying to find out if she'd let it slip to anyone. Which she hadn't.

"How many times do I have to tell you

that I have told no one before you will believe me? Then again, someone who lies for
a living probably wouldn't know the truth if
it slapped him in the face."

Alexander sighed. "I get it. And I believe
you when you say you haven't told anyone.
But is there any way someone could have
come across papers you have, or copies of
the agreement the investigator wanted you
to sign?"

Fine. If he wanted to play this game, she'd
bite.

"I have nothing. The investigator took the
agreement with him when he left. I was home
alone when he came, and I was about ready
to go to my mom's house to sit with her. No
one else was around. Sam was spending the
night at Ryan's so I could take care of my
mom when the nurse went home."

She hated how well she knew the thoughtful look on his face. She could tell he was
processing information, trying to understand.

"What about your friends from college?
Are you in touch with any of them? Any of
them know about you and Bucky?"

Janie shook her head. "No. I had a few
friends, but no one very close. Most of them
warned me off about Bucky, and when I
found out they were right, I was too embar-

rassed to admit it. I left school, and didn't stay in touch with anyone."

Funny, she hadn't thought about most of those people in a long time. Sad to think that none of them had gotten in touch with her, or tried to see how she was doing.

"Who knew you were pregnant?" Alexander asked.

It was strange, going back to a time she'd just as soon forget.

"No one. I didn't realize I was pregnant until just before summer break, and I never went back. No one on my end can connect me to Bucky."

Put that way, it sounded kind of sad.

Alexander looked like he wanted to reach out to her and offer comfort, as he'd done so many times before, but he must've caught her glare because he took a step back.

"What about Bucky and his friends? Did you get to know them while you were dating?"

She didn't have to stand here and answer his questions, but it felt good to finally let it all out. And there was a small part of her that wanted him to know the truth, not whatever lies had been told about her.

"Not really. I was dumb enough to believe Bucky when he said that what we had was special, and that he wasn't ready to tell his friends because they were jerks and they didn't understand what real love was."

She looked at Alexander. Even now, she wasn't sure she knew how to tell the difference between reality and fantasy. Unlike Bucky, at least Alexander had warned her. He'd been telling her all along that things weren't what they seemed, but it hadn't occurred to her just how wrong everything was.

"I'm sorry," Alexander said. "I can't imagine how painful that must be. I know it doesn't feel like it right now, but I'm on your side. I was hoping you could give me some clue as to who might be blackmailing the senator using your name. It sounds like I'm back to square one."

Then he shook his head. "I truly am sorry for the pain I caused you. And I will get to the bottom of this. Regardless of what you think of him, the senator doesn't deserve to be blackmailed. He's a good man, trying to do the right thing for the country."

Janie tried not to laugh bitterly, but she didn't succeed.

"A good man? Boy, does he have you fooled. Do you know what happened when I told Bucky I was pregnant?"

She didn't wait for an answer before continuing. "He threw a hundred-dollar bill at me and told me to take care of it. I went to his father because I thought that his family would want to know about a potential grandchild. He asked me how much money it would take to get me to go away. I didn't take his money then, and I'm not taking his money now."

It felt good to get that out. To remind herself of the inner strength that had been guiding her all these years. She didn't care what Alexander thought of her. Looking at the disappointment on his face, she had to wonder if perhaps he was one of the ones misled by the senator as well.

"Let me ask you something," Janie said. "How close are you to the senator?"

Alexander shrugged. "I work for him. But I wouldn't call him a friend, if that's what you're asking. We don't socialize outside work events, but I don't socialize with many of my coworkers."

He sounded awkward, like the questions made him uncomfortable. And maybe they should. Maybe what he needed to do was examine the senator's motivations in the situation.

"Does he often send you on special projects like this one to search out his son's baby mama?"

Alexander shrugged. "As far as I know, you're the only one. This isn't common knowledge around the office. I think only his closest aides know about this, and I couldn't even tell you which ones."

In a way, Alexander was describing exactly what it felt like to be Bucky's girlfriend. He'd made her feel like their relationship was so special, it had to be a secret. Did Alexander think he was special to the senator?

"Until you got the assignment to track me down, would you have considered yourself one of the senator's closest advisers?" she asked.

Alexander looked confused, but then he said, "No, I guess I wouldn't. This assignment was a promotion. The senator said he was impressed with all the work I've been doing. I was flattered that he thought me capable. I know I let him down by not completing the assignment, but I thought I could do some good here."

It didn't excuse the fact that he'd deceived her, but seeing the disappointment on his face as he put the pieces together to realize that he, too, had been used, made her heart hurt for him. Maybe people like Alexander and the senator could turn off their feelings, but as angry as Janie was, she couldn't simply pretend that she didn't care—but she also didn't need to tell him that.

"Do you think it was just a coincidence that you had family here when you were chosen for this job? Had you told the senator about your connection?"

She hated the expression on his face that told her her point had hit home. Her heart ached for him, and she wished she hadn't been the one to cause him the pain. As much as he'd hurt her, she didn't think it was fair to do the same to him.

"No," he said. "I didn't. I was ashamed of how my family was so broken, and I didn't want to admit that everything wasn't so perfect after all. It didn't occur to me until now that he had me investigated and used what he found to get what he wanted."

"It doesn't feel so good, does it?" she asked. "You were used. Just like you used me. Just like you used everyone else in this town with your helpful act to make them think you were on their side. All to get me to sign some stupid piece of paper that says I'm not going to do what I wasn't going to do already. Was it worth it? All the ways you compromised yourself to get a stupid signature?"

If she'd known she was going to have to go through so much heartbreak over the signature, she would have just signed it when the investigator was there and saved them all a lot of trouble.

"Do you have the agreement?" she asked.

Alexander nodded.

"Get it. I'll sign."

He stared at her like she'd spoken in a different language. But she was done with this nightmare. If they wanted to go to all this trouble to get her signature and give her a bunch of money, fine.

"What about your ability to tell Sam?"

While she longed to tell her son the truth, hopefully he would understand when she told him the lengths of deception his father had gone to to keep him from finding out who he was.

She just wasn't sure how she was going to break it to him that the man he'd hoped would be his dad was cut from the same lying mold. Clearly, in all these years, Janie hadn't learned how to pick a winner.

"I'll tell him as much of the truth as I'm able. Including the part about the lying jerk he asked to be his dad, and his role in it. Sam might not get his father's name from me, but he's a smart kid, and from the details I do share he'll probably figure it out on his own."

Her answer seemed to satisfy Alexander, or

at least he finally realized that arguing would do him no good, because he walked over to the side of the couch and grabbed the folder out of a briefcase, then handed it to her.

"If you don't mind, I'm going to take this and have Ty go over it. Having your best friend married to a lawyer has its perks. I'll be in touch. In the meantime, stay out of my way. If we happen to run into each other, I would appreciate the courtesy of you not trying to engage me."

He nodded slowly, like he understood but didn't like it. What else had he expected? That she'd learn the truth and somehow everything would be okay?

"Thank you," he said. "I truly am sorry."

She didn't believe him, and she knew he didn't expect her to. But she supposed he felt obligated to say the words anyway.

She'd put on a brave face, make her excuses to Ricky, take her son and retreat to Rachel's where, once the kids were put to bed, she could finally confess the pain in her heart to her friend, someone she could count on to never betray her.

Maybe the lesson God was teaching her about opening up was really about recognizing the safe people she had in her life and giving them a chance at her heart. She hadn't been able to talk to her mother, and she regretted it. But it wasn't too late to start with friends like Rachel.

Alexander watched Janie leave, wishing he could call her back and beg her to stay. Part of him wanted to chase after her and take the agreement out of her hands and rip it up, telling her it wasn't worth it.

But it wouldn't win her back, and it wouldn't stop the senator. He'd just send someone else. Ricky and Janie's father entered the den.

"What's wrong with Janie?" Ricky asked. "She said she was fine, but she looked upset when she left here."

Ordinarily, he'd let the other person share their side. But he had to own up to what he'd done. He gestured at the couch before settling in on one of the comfortable chairs.

"Have a seat. It's a long story, and I don't think you're going to like it."

He told them everything, not omitting his role and making it clear that he'd known what he was doing was wrong. Neither man interrupted him, but they listened, letting him tell his side of the story. He supposed it was a good thing Janie's father was a pastor—

maybe he'd show some kindness Alexander didn't deserve.

However, out of courtesy to both the senator and Bucky, but more importantly to Janie, he didn't share the senator's name or Bucky's. He just told both men that he was an important person, and that he wouldn't share the names unless Janie chose to do so.

He didn't care anymore about the senator's privacy. Technically, yes, Alexander had signed a nondisclosure agreement. And part of this probably violated that agreement. But Alexander couldn't live with this on his conscience anymore. He didn't know how Janie had been able to handle keeping it all to herself for so long. It must have been incredibly lonely, and once again, he felt terrible for having earned her trust and betrayed it. It wasn't just the pain of losing her, but of knowing how deeply he'd wounded somebody he genuinely cared about.

He'd known he was going to hurt her; he just hadn't known how badly it would hurt them both.

When he was done telling them what happened, Alexander reached into his pocket for the precious coin Ricky had just given him. He held it out to the older man.

"Here you go, sir. I know I abused your

trust, and I don't deserve this. It meant a lot to me to be part of your family, even if just for a short time."

Ricky brushed his hand away. "The last time I spoke to Cinco, I told him I was ashamed of him. Sometimes at night, those words come back to me, and I would give anything to take them back."

As the old man's eyes teared up, Alexander felt a lump forming in his throat. He'd never intended to hurt anyone, and he hadn't known just how deeply he would feel about it all.

"You keep that coin, son. You're still part of this family. I know you messed up, but there's not one of us who hasn't. Unlike your father, you've chosen to man up and own your mistakes."

Alexander looked down at the coin, studying it, thinking about all the men who'd come before him in the family. He didn't know any of them, but he felt a connection.

"I just wish I knew how to make it better," he said. "Like I told Janie, the man isn't going to give up until he has her signature. I don't believe Janie is guilty of blackmail, but I don't know who else it could be."

He turned to Janie's father. "I believe Janie when she said she didn't tell you any of this. But did you have any idea? Any clue? Could she have said or done anything that would've tipped anyone off?"

Janie's father shook his head. "I'm sorry, but all of this has come as a complete surprise to me. I had no idea she was carrying such a heavy burden, and I wish she would have confided in me."

The sadness on his face made Alexander feel even worse. "I'm sorry if I spoke out of turn. But I wanted to take ownership of the things I have done wrong, even if it means losing the people who have come to be very dear to me."

He sank back in the chair and took a deep breath. "Janie used to tell me all the time about Jesus, how He loves us. I've tried praying, but I don't think it ever worked, not knowing how I was deceiving her. The Lord wouldn't be interested in a guy like me."

He looked up at the pastor. "But I want you to know that she did a really good job. If I weren't such a terrible human being, she would have added to your flock."

His whole life, all he'd wanted to do was help people make a difference. But maybe he didn't know what that was.

"I thought I was doing this for the right reasons," Alexander continued. "I thought doing my job, helping someone I believed could make a real difference and help people, was worth it. And then, when my time came, I would be able to do the same thing. But now I don't know. Is it worth giving up my integrity? All along, I said I had integrity."

He took a deep breath as he remembered all the ways he'd been justifying his deception.

"I told myself that because I never outright lied, just hid the truth or omitted a few facts, that my integrity was intact. But it wasn't. I know that now, and I have to wonder if I'm capable of achieving the great plans I had for the future."

The pastor leaned forward and touched Alexander's arm, just like Janie used to do. "It seems to me that you're exactly the right person for the job. God didn't come to heal the perfect people. He came for the broken, the sick. He wants to mold you, just as you are. The question isn't whether or not you are worthy, but whether or not you're willing to let Him in."

Tears filled Alexander's eyes. His entire life had been about performance. About always doing the right thing.

"I do want to let Him in," Alexander said. "I see the strength Janie has had through all of this, and while I know some of it is because of what an exceptional woman she is,

I also know that a lot of it is from God. Do you think He would give the same strength to me?"

It felt strange, being this vulnerable with the two men before him. He'd spent so many years hiding his weaknesses that sharing them felt wrong. But the more he spoke and shared his heart, the more weight fell off his shoulders.

His life was in shambles. Even if he continued to have a job, he'd lost the trust of the senator, though he wasn't even sure he still wanted it. The woman he loved hated him.

Wait. The woman he loved?

Alexander took a deep breath. Yes. He loved Janie. He was in love for the first time in his life, and he'd messed it up before he'd even had the chance to realize it.

The pastor stood and squeezed Alexander's shoulders. "The Lord gives His mercy to all who ask for it. If you ask for His forgiveness, He will grant it to you, no matter what or how great your sins. And if you ask Him to be part of your life, He will be there."

He looked over at Ricky. "Did you not hear this man's confession?"

Ricky nodded. "Not only did I hear his confession, I heard his deep repentance and his desire to turn to the Lord."

It was strange, hearing acceptance for how badly he'd messed up.

"The question is," the pastor said, "do you believe? The Bible says that if you believe in God and the power of His forgiveness over your sins, then you belong to Him."

His words reminded him of how Janie had been embodying everything she'd spoken to him about the entire time they'd known one another.

"I do," Alexander said. "Now what?"

"Can we pray with you?" the pastor asked.

"I'd like that," Alexander said. "I never understood the power of prayer until now, but I know that the prayers of the people in this community have sustained me, even when I didn't think I believed it. But I do now."

Ricky came over and put his hand on his other shoulder, and both Ricky and Janie's father prayed over Alexander. As their words came over him, he felt the pain and the shame lift away. Though he knew he still had a long way to go in making things right with Janie, and he still didn't know how it would all work out, he felt stronger and more confident of the future than he ever had before.

Chapter Eleven

The upside of having your house burn down and being forced to live with your best friend was that nothing was stopping you from staying up all night talking and having a good cry over getting your heart broken in the worst possible way.

When she'd gotten pregnant with Sam, she had been so ashamed that she hadn't confided in anyone. That, and she hadn't had a close friend like Rachel. So when she confessed everything that had happened, it wasn't just about the situation with Alexander, but how Bucky had betrayed her, how alone she'd felt and how, after all these years, she'd started opening up again only to be betrayed. Even though Janie felt like there was so much left to do today, Rachel had taken the kids and told Janie to spend the day relaxing.

Which she was trying to do as she sat in the kitchen with a cup of coffee.

"Hey, Janie," Ty said, entering the room. He poured himself a cup of coffee, then sat at the table with her.

Last night, she'd managed to mostly keep it together until she got into their cabin and sent the kids into the other room to play. But when she let everything out, she looked like a blubbering fool. At some point she had the presence of mind to hand Ty the nondisclosure agreement and ask him to take a look at it, but still, she felt like the world's biggest idiot.

"How are you feeling today?" he asked.

Janie shrugged. "Embarrassed. I can't believe I came apart like that. And I can't believe I let myself fall for it again."

"None of us saw this coming. He seemed like a great guy," Ty said. He took a sip of his coffee, then looked at her. "And you forget, I knew you back then. Even though I promised you we'd never talk about it again, that night that I saw you out with Bucky, I knew he was a loser. If you recall, I told you that."

Janie nodded. "I know. And you were good enough never to say I told you so when I came home. You were supportive, and I don't think I gave you enough credit for that back then. I was too busy pushing everyone away in my shame."

As much as she'd always thought she'd been completely alone during that time, she did have people like Ty. But she hadn't let him in the way she should have, just like she'd kept a lot of others at arm's length, like her parents.

"What good would it have done for me to do that? You were already hurting, and you didn't need to get beaten up with the truth so I could feel better about the fact that my warning came true. I didn't feel good about that. It felt awful, being right."

He gestured at the folder containing the nondisclosure agreement. "And it feels more awful to have to face this. You should have told me. I know you don't want to be a bother, but this is the kind of stuff you need to rely on your friends for. I have the legal expertise, and you shouldn't be afraid to use it."

That was one of the positive things that had come out of last night. Somehow, in all the tears, she'd found something deep inside her that was tired of being the victim.

"I'm not. From the time I became involved with Bucky until now, he's been the one in control. He would dictate when I got to see him, or if he had time to talk. And then he was the one to end the relationship when he'd gotten what he wanted from me. He controlled whether or not my son had a father, and the fact that I had no support. And now, because his father is running for a higher office, he wants to control that narrative, too. I'm done with that."

She looked over at the papers. "I will sign them, and I will accept his blood money. It's the least he can do after all this time. I can use it to do some good, not just for Sam and me, but it would give the community center some needed funds. But I also want you to go through the agreement with a fine-tooth comb to make sure that it's not just Bucky's interests that are protected, but mine as well."

Ty tapped on the folder. "It's pretty standard. But I'll make sure to be added to this as your attorney on record so that any further communication will go through me. You don't have to put up with this harassment anymore."

It felt good to have an ally. A true ally, not a fake friend like Alexander. Her stomach ached at the thought. She'd truly believed that he cared for her. They'd worked so well together, and she'd thought he was her friend. It was hard looking back on what she thought were genuine moments of connection and wondering how much of it had been real.

"You're a guy. Do you think he actually cared for me?"

He looked thoughtful for a moment, then said, "Honestly, I wouldn't have believed it of him. Until you came in here last night, I would have said I'd never met a more standup guy."

His words made her feel slightly better. Ty was one of the most suspicious people she knew because of his profession. He was even more mistrustful of others than she was, so if he hadn't seen Alexander's deception coming, then maybe she wasn't as hopeless a judge of character after all.

A knock sounded at the door. Ty looked at Janie. "If it's Alexander, do you want me to tell him to go away?"

Janie shrugged. "Just tell him you haven't had time to fully go over the agreement yet, and I will call him when it's ready."

Ty shook his head. "I have a better idea. I'm officially your attorney. Anything he needs to say will go through me, unless you choose to talk to him. I'll handle the agreement, and you just focus on doing what you need to do to feel better."

Hearing Ty's defense of her strengthened

her in a way she hadn't expected. Once again, she was reminded that she didn't have to do this alone. She just wished her mother could have been here to be part of it.

When Ty opened the door, it wasn't Alexander, but her father.

"I wanted to see how you're doing after last night," he said.

Janie smiled at him, wishing she didn't look like such a wreck. Even though she'd told Rachel and Ty, and she'd already promised herself to be more open with others in her life, she wasn't sure she was ready to talk to her father about this.

"I'm sorry I rushed out of there like that," she said. "I had a lot on my mind."

Ty held up a coffee cup. "Would you like some?"

Her father nodded. "Please. I had a long night as well."

He took the cup Ty offered, then joined Janie at the table. "I know what happened between you and Alexander. He told us everything."

Janie stared at him. Everything? She wasn't sure she could believe that. Alexander was a master manipulator who knew how to tell just enough of the truth to make himself look good.

"I hope you're not here to defend him," Ty

said. "Don't you think Janie has been through enough?"

Her father nodded. "She has been through a lot."

Then he turned to Janie. "Which is why I wanted to see if you're okay. I can't imagine how difficult all of this must have been for you, having a powerful man and his son coming after you. Alexander didn't tell us who they were, but they must be pretty powerful to have both of you so scared."

Scared? Janie half laughed at the thought of Alexander being scared. "He was just doing his job," she said.

Her father nodded. "He was. And while I'm not here to defend Alexander's actions, I want you to know that all the things you said to him had an impact. He accepted Christ last night, and I believe that God was working in his heart the entire time."

"You believe him?" Ty asked.

Her father nodded. "I do. My point of sharing that isn't to try to convince you to see things from his side, but to let you know that the time you spent with him wasn't in vain. I know what happened hurts, and I pray that God will give you the healing you need. But I hope you find a little comfort in the fact that some of what you went through, God used for good."

Funny that that was the first part of the Bible Janie had ever quoted to Alexander. The worst part was, hearing God's word, especially as it applied to her situation, made it almost impossible to hold a grudge.

"I suppose I'm expected to just forgive him, is that it?" she asked.

Her father put his arm around her. "I didn't say that. Joseph didn't forgive his brothers overnight. It was a process, just like you're going to have to figure out whatever process it will take for you to get through this. And you will get through this."

He hugged her tight to him and kissed her on top of the head. "And I hope, this time, you will let us be there for you through it."

Once again, she was reminded of the fact that all the times she'd thought she was on her own, she didn't have to be. Her father loved her, just as Rachel and Ty did.

"I know," Janie said. "I just wish Mom were here so I could tell her that, too. So many times the past couple of weeks, I've wanted to talk to her about this. I hate that it took me until it's too late to realize that."

Her father hugged her again. "I'm sure she knew how much we loved her, and that's what matters. I miss her, too. We've kept busy with the fire recovery efforts, saying it's what she would have wanted, and what she would have done. But she also believed in a time for everything, and we haven't taken our time to mourn. So how about you go get dressed, we'll drive to that little café she liked in Storm Valley, and let's spend the day together, mourning your mother, mourning the past and mourning your feelings about Alexander."

All this time, Janie had been avoiding her feelings. Everyone kept telling her she needed to deal with them, and as she looked at the light in her father's eyes and saw the love he felt for her, she knew it was time.

"Sounds good," she said. Even though what she wanted to do most was find some way to stay busy to avoid dealing with all of this, everyone was right. She'd have breakfast with her father, mourn her mother and deal with the pain of losing so much all at once.

As much as Alexander wanted to fix things with Janie, both her father and Ricky had told him to give her space. But they still had a Thanksgiving dinner to plan, and since the senator had been unwilling to consider his idea, Alexander needed to find turkeys for the community. Part of him just wanted to turn tail and go home now, but he'd made a commitment to the community, and the senator had given him until after Thanksgiving. It would also allow him time to think about who could be blackmailing the senator.

He went through the file again, looking for clues. The address on the envelope, as well as the one the senator was directed to send payments to, was a PO box here in Columbine Springs. Thankfully, the post office hadn't suffered any damage from the fire, being on the opposite end of the town.

Even though it was technically against postal code for them to give out information about box holders, maybe the sweet lady who worked at the post office, Cheryl, could help him figure out a way to identify the person without breaking the law.

It felt weird driving into town without Janie. She'd been his constant companion the past couple weeks, and she and Sam always had interesting ways to keep him entertained on the drive. He prayed again for wisdom on how to handle the situation, and promised that if God would be so merciful as to give him a second chance with her, then Alexander would spend the rest of his life making it up to her.

As he turned the corner leading to the post office, he saw a familiar figure entering.

Janie?

He parked the truck and went in. Janie's back was to him as she went through the PO box. Even at a distance, he could tell it was the same box number as the one that had appeared in all of the blackmail letters. But as he got closer, he realized that while the woman's shape was similar to Janie's, it wasn't her.

Though the woman wore a hat and a large coat, they were clearly designer, not the off brands Janie tended to wear. So who was this woman?

"Excuse me," he said, tapping her on the shoulder. She turned, and though her face was shielded with large sunglasses, he recognized her immediately.

Corrine, Bucky's fiancée.

Alexander had never met her in person, but he'd seen her from a distance and seen enough photos of her that he knew who she was. She and Bucky had been on-again off-again for years, but with the election coming up, they'd formalized things with an engagement.

"Corrine? What are you doing here?"

She stared down her glasses at him. "Do I know you?"

"Not exactly, no. I'm just surprised to see you here."

She shrugged. "Just running errands for a friend." She held up a stack of envelopes. "But they're all junk. It seems I wasted my time."

He stared at her, hard. "He's not going to send any more money until he gets a signed nondisclosure agreement. Did you think about that?"

The startled expression on her face told him all he needed to know. Before he could ask any more questions, Bucky burst into the post office.

"Did you get it? We've got to go. We're going to be late to Dad's fund-raiser if we don't hurry."

Then Bucky stopped and stared at him. "Do I know you?"

Alexander nodded. "I'm the man your father hired to get Janie's signature on the nondisclosure agreement so she would stop blackmailing him. But she's not the one blackmailing him, is she?"

He watched as Bucky and Corrine exchanged nervous glances, but then Corrine shrugged. "You might as well tell him. He's right about your dad not sending any more money until she signs that stupid agreement.

Why did he have to send someone to do it in person? He was supposed to just mail it to her so we could forge a signature and get that money."

"Shut up, Corrine," Bucky said.

Alexander couldn't help the disgusted look he gave Bucky. "Why would you do that? You have everything. All this time, you've been close enough to visit your son and get to know him, and all you cared about was stealing your father's money?"

Bucky shrugged. "He keeps cutting my allowance every time I mess up. Corrine has certain needs, and you honestly think I can afford her wardrobe, let alone her spa visits, on the pitiful salary my father gives me? This is really his fault. If he wants me to have a trophy wife like Corrine, then he should pay for it."

Alexander looked at Corrine to see how she felt about being treated like an object, but she simply stared at her nails like she was bored.

"What? A woman's got needs. Bucky's father didn't used to be so stingy."

The two of them disgusted him. How could Janie have fallen for such a piece of pond scum?

"I suppose you're going to tell my father, aren't you?" Bucky asked.

Alexander shrugged. "You'll make up some kind of lie. But so that you know, I've gotten her to agree to sign the nondisclosure agreement. Your father will have it on his desk after Thanksgiving, and Janie will receive the final payment for your blackmail scheme. You're going to have to find a new way of financing your lifestyle."

Corrine stomped over to Bucky and gave him a shove. "This is all your fault. If you hadn't gotten greedy with that last letter, none of this would've happened."

The two continued bickering as they walked out the door. Alexander was glad to be rid of them, and even more glad that he finally had an explanation for the blackmail, but it only made him feel worse at the thought of how wrong he'd misjudged Janie. She was one of the few truly good people he'd met in his life.

Actually, that wasn't fair to the people he knew. He'd met many good people here in Columbine Springs. His parents were good people, even his mother. The forgiveness he'd received last night in prayer had made him realize that just as God forgave him, he needed to forgive his mother on a deeper level. She'd done the best she could, and her misstep did not discount the fact that she'd been the best mom in the world.

Now to figure out what to do for Janie. He wanted her to be able to tell Sam the truth when he was old enough. Because she was right. The damage the lies had done to Alexander and William wasn't anything Sam deserved.

As for the money, Alexander felt that Janie deserved it. But he could also understand why she didn't want to accept it.

As he turned to leave, Cheryl came out from behind the counter.

"I didn't fully understand everything that was going on there, but am I right to understand that those people were trying to cause trouble for Janie?"

Alexander nodded. "Not trying, I'm afraid. They are. I hate to drag you into the middle of all this, but if it comes down to it, would you be willing to testify about what you saw?"

Cheryl grinned. "Of course I will. But I've got something even better. A while back, some kids were vandalizing the post office. So I installed some cameras to find out who it was."

She pointed to a sign in the lobby warning people they were under surveillance. "I got the whole thing on tape. And it's legal, too, because of my sign. Those boys think they can come to my town and vandalize my post office? I don't think so. I kept my cameras up, just in case they come back."

Which meant she could have a surveillance video of the previous blackmail attempts as well.

"How long do those videos go back?" he asked. "How long do you keep them for?"

Cheryl looked at him like he was an idiot. "I keep everything. You never know when you're going to need it. So I can give you footage for up to two years back. You're welcome."

Cheryl puffed up her chest. "Just wait until I tell Norm. He thinks I'm crazy for how long I keep stuff. This probably helps you out a lot, doesn't it?"

Trying not to laugh, Alexander said, "It does. Let me get a list of dates for you, and we can check the tapes to see if they have anything I need."

"I'll make a copy for you of what happened here."

Excited that he might have found a way out of this mess for Janie, he drove back to the ranch. Janie's father had asked him to give Janie some space, and Alexander figured he could talk to her when he saw her to get the papers.

But when he entered the main ranch house, Ty stepped out of Ricky's office area.

"Good. You're back. Come in here and have a chat."

He hadn't spent much time talking with Ty, but his reputation as an attorney preceded him. Janie had told him she was going to have Ty look over the agreement.

"I want to talk to you as well."

The surprise on the other man's face told Alexander everything he needed to know. Ty was on Janie's side. And that was okay. At this point, he figured Janie probably wouldn't forgive him. She had no reason to trust him. Regardless, he was going to do the right thing by her. Once they were in Ty's office, Ty closed the door behind him.

"Well," he began. "What do you want to talk about?"

Alexander spied the nondisclosure agreement on Ty's desk. Janie had followed through with her threat to have him look it over, but Alexander wasn't worried about that. At least now, Ty could help him draft an alternative agreement. As a lawyer, he'd have spotted any potential traps in the agreement, and could also figure out ways to make the new agreement even stronger.

"I need you to redraft the nondisclosure agreement."

Ty grinned. "Done. You don't think I'd let her sign something that didn't give her extra protection, do you?"

Everyone said Ty was a good lawyer, and were Alexander not on Janie's side, it would have been more problematic. But this worked in his favor, even if Ty didn't realize it yet.

"Fire up your computer and be prepared to make more changes," Alexander said. "I've just come across new information that's going to be a game-changer for Janie. She didn't want to sign because she didn't want to take away Sam's right to know who his father is. Not only does she not have to, but I don't want her to. As far as I'm concerned, Janie holds all the cards, and by the time this agreement is done, the senator will be willing to sign whatever she asks."

Ty's eyes narrowed. "Don't think that you can play me as easily as you played Janie or her father. Pastor Roberts is a good man, and I can understand why he would want to believe in your repentance. But I know men like you. I've been in courtrooms with bigger sharks than the senator, and I have always won."

If Alexander had anything to be afraid of, he'd be shaking in his boots. But he wasn't worried about Ty. He'd already lost everything important to him.

"Bucky is the one blackmailing the senator."

Ty stared at him. "How do you know that? Do you have proof?"

"I caught him red-handed at the post office with his fiancée, who has been posing as Janie. Better yet, Cheryl has the place under video surveillance, which means I have it all on tape. The senator doesn't have a leg to stand on, not if he wants to protect his precious boy."

It was almost funny, watching the incredulous look deepen on Ty's face. "Just whose side are you on, anyway?"

Alexander shrugged. "Janie's. I was wrong to do what I did to her. She didn't deserve that. And she doesn't deserve what's happening to her now."

"So you think you're going to win her back?" Ty asked.

At this point, Alexander knew he didn't have a chance. "I ruined everything with her. I get that. But there are some wrongs I can make right, and that's what I'm here to do. Now are you listening, or not?"

"What about your job?" Ty asked. "From what Janie said, it was everything to you."

Alexander nodded. "It was. Until Janie taught me that there are things more important than my job. I have no doubt that I'll lose it as a result of this, if I haven't already. I have some connections, but I don't know that this is the work I want to do anymore. Ricky said he'd find something for me at the ranch for a while. But I don't want to be a burden on him, either. So I'm just going to play it by ear for now, and once I get this agreement handled and we get through Thanksgiving, I'll figure it out."

As aimless as it sounded, it felt good to admit that he didn't have a plan. Strange, because his entire life had been built around this idea that he was going to someday be president of the United States. But the more he thought about the senator, and the moral compromises he had to make to get even this far, the more Alexander wasn't sure he wanted that. The happiest he'd been in his entire life was here, helping the people in Columbine Springs.

"You're serious, aren't you?" Ty asked.

Alexander nodded. "I asked the senator

to help with the turkeys they needed for the Thanksgiving celebration, and he refused, because it isn't that big of a voter base. I don't want those to be the types of choices I have to make."

Ty nodded slowly, like the changes Alexander was making in his life were finally sinking in. He wasn't the same man who'd arrived in Columbine Springs three weeks ago. The fire had changed him. God had changed him.

More importantly, Janie had changed him.

"I guess we'd better get to work then," Ty said.

As he went around his desk to his laptop, Alexander felt even more weight fall off his shoulders. No, he didn't know what the future held for him, but at least he knew that the agreement they were about to work out was going to be in Janie and Sam's best interests.

Chapter Twelve

"Why hasn't Mr. Alexander come to see us today?" Sam asked.

How were you supposed to tell a child about the complexities of grown-up relationships that didn't work out? This was one of the main reasons she didn't date. How did you do so when it wasn't just your heart that was involved?

"He's been busy," Janie said.

It was a copout, and she knew it, but she didn't know what else to say.

"Well, he said he'd always be there for me. I'm going to get my paper and call him."

That was the last thing she needed now.

"Sweetheart, Alexander and I had a fight and even though he promised you that he'd always be there for you, I need a break. Can you give it a little time before you call him?"

Hopefully, it would be enough time for her to figure out how to explain to her son that Alexander was a jerk, and she didn't want him in Sam's life.

"I think you need to work it out. That's what you always tell me and Katie and Ryan. Maybe you need to see things from his side. And even if you think you are right, and he is wrong, is it really worth losing your best friend over?"

It was hard not to laugh at her son parroting her words. How many times had she given that exact speech to the kids over one of their petty disagreements? But she and Alexander weren't kids, and this wasn't a petty disagreement. Alexander had lied to her. Used her. Betrayed her trust. And while her father said he believed that Alexander was truly repentant, her heart was too fragile to let him back in.

"I understand what you're saying," Janie said. "But this is a grown-up issue. Please give Mommy some time, okay?"

Sam put his hands on his hips and gave her the sternest look a seven-year-old could muster. "Fine. You can have a time-out. But you better not take too long, because then you'd better say you're sorry and hug and make up. You're always telling me that God wants us to forgive each other. So you better do what God says."

At least she knew her son had been listening. But how could she get him to understand that some problems couldn't be fixed?

Yes, she knew she had an obligation to forgive Alexander, not just because the Bible told her to, but also because she knew it was necessary for her peace of mind. But as her father said, it didn't have to happen right at this moment. Still, she knew the longer she held on to her grudge, the harder it would be. She didn't know how to balance her feelings with what was right.

"I will consult God on it," Janie told her son. "But you need to mind your own business. So let grown-ups handle the grown-up issues, and when the time is right, I'll let you call Alexander."

The disappointment on Sam's face tore Janie's heart in two. It was so unfair, the heartbreak her son also had to endure. She hoped it was worth it for Alexander. Because she was going to be cleaning up this mess for a long time.

The front door opened, and Katie burst through, Ty following.

"You're home early," Janie said. "Rachel isn't back from her errands yet."

Ty set his briefcase on the table. "That's okay. I finished what I was working on early, and I got a new agreement drafted that I wanted to discuss with you."

She looked over at where the kids had made quick work of pulling out a puzzle and were already working on it at the coffee table.

"Why don't you guys go into Katie's room and play with her train set," Janie suggested.

Sam groaned and looked at Katie. "Mom and Alexander are having a fight, which means she wants to talk to your dad about it in private."

Then he turned and glared at Janie. "But I hope Ty tells you that you have to forgive him and make up so he can be my dad."

Wow. This was way more serious than she'd thought.

She took a deep breath and asked God for an extra measure of wisdom and patience. "And I told you to leave the grown-up matters to grown-ups. God also says you're supposed to obey your mother, so maybe you need to spend a little bit of time talking to Him about that."

Sam's face fell, and she wished this would be the last disappointment he'd have concerning Alexander. She hadn't realized how firmly he'd had his heart set on having Alexander as a father.

"Fine," Sam said. "But me and Katie are also going to go in there and pray for me to get my dad. You're being selfish to stay mad at him."

The kids stomped off with such indignation that Janie would have laughed, if she weren't on the verge of heartbreak. It wasn't just Sam who was hurt by all this. But what was she supposed to do? Tell a pathological liar that everything he'd done to hurt her was okay?

Ty walked over and squeezed her shoulders. "I'm sorry. I hate that the kids think they brought Rachel and me together with their prayers. Now they think they can do the same for you, and I know it's not that simple."

Janie brushed away a stray tear. "You mean once Sam got over the fact that you became Katie's dad, not his. I just don't know how to get him to understand that as much as he wants a dad, it's not that simple."

"Relationships are complicated," Ty said. "And I know you don't want anyone else butting in on the situation with you and Alexander, but I think you should know that he and I worked together to craft a new agreement that's more favorable to you. I know this doesn't fix everything between the two of you, and you have a long way to go, but—"

"Stop. I know everyone means well, but just give me the papers, and I will sign them. I need this part of my life to be over. As for Alexander, I need you to leave me alone where he's concerned and let me handle it in my own way."

She hated the disappointment that washed over Ty's face, but he nodded. "I understand. It was probably too soon for me to push you in that direction, anyway. But I hope, once you've taken time to sort through your feelings, you read through this agreement and understand that almost all the changes were his idea, not mine."

She barely glanced at the papers he handed her. "But you agree with them?"

"I do," he said. "The senator still has to sign them, but Alexander thinks he can get him to, and I agree with his plan."

Janie grabbed a pen. "That's all I need to know, then. You might be trying to fix things between Alexander and me, but I know you wouldn't steer me wrong legally." She initialed each page, then signed where it indicated.

She wasn't kidding when she said she wanted this over with. With every stroke of the pen, she felt a little bit freer at knowing that because of this document, no one else was going to be waiting in the wings, trying to destroy the life she'd built.

When she finished signing, she handed the papers back to Ty. "We didn't talk about the money, but even though I said I was willing to accept it, I don't want any of the senator's hush money. Can you make arrangements to donate it to the community resource center anonymously? Even though Alexander thinks I can handle the executive director position, I spent a lot of time looking at the information Ellen gave me, as well as some of the documents and websites he pointed me toward. I'm not qualified for the job, but this money will help us find someone who is."

Ty looked down at the papers for a moment, then back at her. "I can do some of that. But one of the changes Alexander insisted on was that in addition to the money you get now, there's also money put away in a college fund for Sam. He wants Sam to be taken care of, no matter what happens."

It shouldn't have surprised her that Alexander would think of Sam. As much as she didn't want to admit it, the one thing she knew for certain was that he genuinely cared for her son. But given Alexander's loyalty to the senator, she would have thought that he'd have tried to save his boss as much as possible.

"That was sweet of him, but unnecessary. Still, I might as well take it. One less thing for me to worry about, right?"

The look Ty gave her told her she probably didn't want to know what he was about to say, but she was going to have to hear it anyway.

"You realize this will probably cost him his job, right?" Ty gave her the same disappointed look Sam had. "Again, I realize that you aren't ready to work through this, and that's fine. But you do need to get to a place where you can hear him out, and understand other developments to the situation."

She shook her head. "So it's okay that he hurt me?"

"I didn't say that," Ty said. "What he did was wrong, and we all know it. But you have to find a way to let go of your pain."

"I just need time," she said.

"You got it," he said, stuffing the papers back into his briefcase. "I'm going to go run these back to Alexander so he can get them to the senator. He wants this taken care of by Thanksgiving, so he can enjoy the community celebration. You don't mind watching both kids for a little bit, do you?"

Janie shook her head. She hadn't considered that Alexander would stay around for Thanksgiving. "He's still planning on coming?"

"Yes," Ty said. "He's put a lot of effort into making it happen and, at Shelley's suggestion, is going to try to get the rest of his family to come."

His face softened, then he said, "I realize it's going to be hard for you to face him then, and maybe that's why we're trying to push you more in the direction of forgiveness. You two worked hard as a team to help this community, and you both should enjoy the reward of everyone coming together to celebrate triumphing over everything we've lost."

Without waiting for an answer, Ty left Janie alone to consider what all of this meant. Alexander had shattered her heart into a million little pieces, and while everyone in her life said they supported her, they kept trying to push her back to him. Why?

She got up and went to Katie's room where she peeked in on the kids, who were rewatching Rachel and Ty's wedding video. Katie loved it so much that Rachel had put it on the tablet for her to watch whenever she wanted. Tears sprang to her eyes as she realized the intensity on Sam's face as he watched Ty promise to be Katie's dad forever.

If Janie were honest with herself, she'd admit that watching Ty and Rachel find happiness had put a little hope in her heart that maybe she could find it for herself as well. Then meeting Alexander and seeing all the ways he'd brought her walls down had caused that hope to grow.

So was everyone pushing them back together just more wishful thinking, or was there a chance...

No. She wasn't going to let herself go there again.

Alexander strode into the senator's office, papers in hand. A group of aides surrounded him, going over some document. Alexander didn't care.

"Do you have an appointment?" one of them asked.

Alexander ignored the question. "I have the signature you requested, sir," he said. "And regarding that signature, we have another matter to discuss."

The senator waved away his aides. "Give us some privacy please."

Once the room was clear and the door closed behind them, Alexander handed the senator the agreement. "As you can see, she's fully executed the document, with the assistance of her attorney."

The senator took the papers, and immediately noticed they were different. "This isn't the document I sent you to have her sign."

Alexander shook his head. "No, it isn't. Her attorney and I redrafted it. You see, as I told you, she was not behind the blackmail. Bucky and Corrine were. Corrine has been posing as Janie, using the post office at Columbine Springs to send and receive the blackmail notes and money."

The senator threw the papers to the ground. "That's preposterous. How dare you come in here and make such accusations?"

Alexander pulled out a copy of the video of Bucky and Corrine in the post office. Cheryl had also managed to find footage of a couple of other visits Corrine had made to the post office.

"I have them on video. Here's how this is going to work. You're going to sign that agreement without argument, without changes, and you will do everything exactly as laid out in it. That includes paying Janie the full amount promised, as well as setting up a college fund for Sam."

The senator glared at him. "Are you blackmailing me?"

Alexander shook his head. "Not yet. Not if you sign that document."

Then he pulled out another one. "And this is the agreement terminating my employment. I already knew you were going to fire me. So this grants me a termination with a generous severance package, and the understanding that you will not badmouth me in the future."

The senator laughed. "Do you honestly think I'm going to sign either one of them? Even if I were so inclined, I would have my lawyers go over them with a fine-tooth comb first."

Alexander shrugged. "You can. But if I don't have them fully executed and in my possession within twenty-four hours, this video is going to the press. My lawyer went over the nondisclosure agreement I signed as a condition of my employment with you. While there are certain things I'm not allowed to talk about, nothing is prohibiting me from discussing the findings of my investigation into your blackmail. Were I to make this information public, the police would be very interested in the fact that you were being blackmailed. Corrine and Bucky would both be under investigation for blackmail as well as identity theft, considering they were impersonating Janie. There's also the fraud committed with her cashing the checks. But do consult your lawyers. You have twenty-four hours."

The senator pulled out his phone and punched in a few numbers. "George. We've got a problem."

Alexander figured he'd call his attorney, and when George Johnson entered the senator's office, Alexander was glad to have another witness who would understand that he meant business.

The senator gave George a rundown of what was happening, then George looked over at Alexander. "You realize you're making serious accusations."

"Watch the video. I'd say talk to Bucky, but I'm sure he'll lie. I think the video will speak for itself."

It didn't take more than a minute or so of footage before the senator closed his laptop.

"Who else has copies of this?"

Alexander shrugged. "Me, my lawyer and the postmaster at the Columbine Springs post office. She takes record-keeping very seriously and never throws anything away. She loves Janie like a daughter, and she was very concerned that someone would try to hurt her. Not only does she have the tape, but she witnessed the whole thing, so it's up to you what you'd like to do with that information."

George whispered something in the senator's ear, then the senator nodded.

"And if I sign these agreements, the videos will never see the light of day?"

Alexander gestured at the documents. "Page fourteen. You abide by the agreements, and no one ever has to know. But the second you are in violation, every media news outlet will get a copy."

"Give me a few minutes' privacy with my lawyer," the senator said.

"Fine," Alexander said. "It'll give me the chance to clear my desk and say goodbye."

When he got to his desk, it had already been taken over by another campaign worker.

"Do you know what happened to the stuff that was in this desk before you came?" Alexander asked.

The guy nodded. "Oh yeah, sure. It's in a box in the break room. Was it your desk? I'm sorry. They told me no one was using it, so I could have it."

The guy's response was all Alexander needed to confirm that he'd made the right decision. He already knew what would be in the box. Just a few personal items, but nothing of significance. And as he looked around at the people in the office, he realized that not one of them had come over even to say hello or that they'd missed him. The truth was every single one of them had dreams of becoming president or senator or holding some other political office, and this was just one stepping stone. The people they met here were competition, or perhaps future contacts, but no one they cared about.

Ty had told him that Janie had no intention of applying for the director position at the community resource center, and that she'd asked him to set up a trust for all the senator's money to go to helping fund the kind of director the center needed.

That was the kind of job Alexander wanted. And even though he knew it would make Janie uncomfortable, he was going to apply. If he didn't get it, he'd find a job somewhere else, doing something similar. But he hoped he could make it work. In just a few short weeks, Columbine Springs had become his home, and the people of the town his family. Regardless of the outcome, he'd learned how he could make a difference in people's lives, and even though it wouldn't be through politics, he knew he was going to make the world a better place.

A few minutes later, George came out of

the senator's office. "The senator signed everything just as you asked."

After Alexander examined each page to make sure everything was in order, he went to the copy room he'd been in so many times before, and made copies of everything for both him and the senator, keeping the originals.

"My lawyer will be checking in to make sure everything is done as promised."

George nodded. "It will be." He paused slightly. "He knew Bucky wasn't the greatest human being. But he truly didn't realize just how far he'd fallen. Until today, the senator believed everything Bucky said about Janie. He believed Janie was blackmailing him. I don't blame you for protecting Janie's interests or your own, but I hope you know that the senator truly does have good intentions for our state and our country."

Alexander nodded. "So did I. But I'm no longer willing to compromise my morals to get there. And I found way more satisfaction in being part of a grassroots effort to help the people than anything I've ever done here. If the senator truly wants to make a difference, then he should spend time with the people he says he's here to serve."

George gave him a blank look, like he thought Alexander's words were those of an idealistic kid straight out of college. And that was okay. He didn't need the approval of George, the senator or anyone but God to know that he was on the right path.

God had answered his prayers about Janie's situation, and the results were far better than he could've ever imagined. But as he left the senator's office, he prayed that, even though Alexander didn't deserve it, God would bring him and Janie back together again.

Chapter Thirteen

Janie smoothed her dress as she looked around Ricky's dining hall on Thanksgiving Day. Everyone was gathered for the dinner, but she hadn't seen Alexander yet. Maybe he had chickened out. She certainly had had her moments this morning while getting ready. But she thought a lot about what everyone had told her, even though she'd pretty much dismissed them all and pushed them away, and she'd been putting together some of the pieces in her head.

If Alexander had done everything to hurt her for the sake of his job, then risked losing it to help her, maybe his heart had changed. Her father had said he accepted Christ, which meant he was a new person. Mixed in with all her thoughts of how angry she'd been at him were the memories of how wonderful he'd been.

He couldn't have faked the way he loved her community members. The way he loved her son.

But more than that, she thought about what Alexander had said about never lying to her. Try as she might, she couldn't find a single lie he'd told. In some ways, that was how she'd justified all the secrets she'd kept over the years. Was it fair to hold Alexander to a higher standard?

He'd even warned her that things weren't what they seemed, but she'd fallen in love with him anyway.

Yes, she'd admit it. She'd fallen in love.

Janie didn't know how she was going to face him.

Maybe everyone had told him that her heart was so hardened against him that he shouldn't come. And now, more than anything, she wished he had. If only for him to see the fruits of their labors. And maybe afterward, they could talk, and she could hear his side of things and sort through the emotions in her heart. She missed him, and while she didn't know what to do with that fact, every time she prayed about the situation, she heard the verse in Genesis she'd spoken to him when they first met going through her head.

Had Alexander not come to Columbine Springs, the Petersons would have lost all of the animals and all of their personal belongings, and countless others wouldn't have had their lives touched by Alexander. He'd come for the wrong reasons, and he could've left, to try again another day, but he'd stayed.

All was not what it had seemed, and Janie had to trust that God had some kind of plan, even if she didn't understand it.

Shelley approached her, smiling. "Everything looks wonderful. Your mother would be so proud."

"Thanks to you and your bunco group," Janie said, hugging the other woman.

"Speaking of the bunco group, we have a little something for you." Shelley handed her a large gift bag.

When Janie looked inside, she saw it held a giant binder.

"We can't replace the one you lost, but we put together one of our own, writing down everything we could think of. Some of the ladies even had a few notes from Bette, so we put those in there as well. With each holiday and event, we'll help you add to that binder, so eventually, you'll have replaced everything you lost. I know it's not the same, but—"

Janie pulled Shelley into another hug. "It's even better. Thank you."

Funny how, now that she'd spent time dealing with her grief, the pain of not having her mother around didn't feel so unbearable. Yes, she wished with everything in her heart that she could be here with them, but she knew her mother's legacy would live on.

"All right, now. I've got food to serve," Shelley said, pulling away.

Sam came running toward them.

"Mr. Alexander is here. And you'll never guess. There is a guy who looks just like him."

Janie had heard that Alexander was going to try to bring his family, though in all of her conversations with him, he sounded pretty hopeless that his brother would ever come around.

Before she could process that information, Alexander walked through the door with an older couple, trailed by a man who looked just like him, as Sam had said. His family had come after all. Tears clogged the back of Janie's throat as Sam tugged at her leg. "We have to go say hi."

Her feet felt glued to the floor, but just

when she thought she might have the strength to move, the senator walked in as well.

She just stood there, staring. What was going on here?

Alexander walked right up to her. "Everything looks wonderful," he said. "I'm sorry I didn't help these last few days, but I had other things to attend to."

He gestured at the older couple. "These are my parents, Bill and Mary. And I'm sure you've figured out that this is William, my twin. I know I'm probably the last person on earth that you want to see, but I did want you to at least meet them. They've heard a lot about you and the difference you've made in my life, but you don't have to entertain them."

This was definitely not what she was expecting. She didn't know how she was going to get a moment to speak with him about what was on her mind with his family here.

Alexander turned to Sam. "I'm sorry I haven't been around, buddy. But I did some things to hurt your mom, so I needed time to fix what I broke. It doesn't make what I did right, but I am trying to do the right thing now."

Then Alexander looked over at his brother, who handed him a bag. "I'm not very good with tools and things," Alexander said. "But my brother is. So I asked him to fix your dump truck. I hope he did a good job."

Sam looked in the bag and squealed with delight. "It's better than ever! I have to go show Katie and Ryan."

He took the bag and ran off.

Janie's heart felt like it was going to burst at how deep Alexander's concern for Sam ran. She hadn't been wrong about how he cared for her son. Maybe they really could find a way to start over.

Except somehow, Alexander had managed to drag the senator here as well. How was this part of the efforts to make things right?

Alexander's parents stepped aside, and the senator and his wife came forward.

"This is Senator James Blackwell and his wife, Anne," Alexander said. "They donated the turkeys for today's feast."

"I told you, those were supposed to be anonymous," the senator said.

Alexander shrugged. "She's been tirelessly helping me plan this, so as one of the planners, I felt she had the right to know. I refuse to keep any more secrets from Janie."

The senator nodded slowly. "All right then." He turned his attention to Janie, bringing her back to when she was a scared college girl, trying to get the family to do the right thing.

"I wanted to tell you in person that I'm sorry. I believed the lies my son told about you. And I'm ashamed to say I've kept all this from my wife. She didn't know until she heard me yelling at Bucky about him blackmailing me in your name. I've made a lot of mistakes, and I don't know how to begin to atone for them," he said, looking over at his wife.

Tears were in his eyes, and Janie almost felt bad for him, especially because of the hurt way his wife looked at him.

"I didn't know about Sam," the senator's wife said. "I know my husband and son behaved abominably, but I hope you will consider, in time, letting me get to know him."

The senator nudged her, and she added, "Even though he doesn't deserve it, I hope at some point you might consider letting Jim in, as well."

The poor woman was practically shaking, and her eyes were filled with tears. Janie opened her arms to her and hugged her. "I know what it's like to be betrayed by someone you love, and just like you, I'm working through forgiving that. But I think the beauty of God's love is the grace God gives us, and the grace we need to give each other. I would love for you to be part of Sam's life. I'm going to need some time to adjust and to explain to him, but you are his grandmother, and if God saw fit to bring you here today, who am I to keep you from him?"

As she spoke the healing words over the older woman sobbing in her arms, she felt a peace in her heart that she hadn't felt since before her mother died.

At that moment, she forgave Alexander. And once again, it hit home just how much of this had been brought about by his mistakes.

After they finished hugging, Janie turned to Alexander. "Thank you. When I first met you, I told you the story of Joseph, and I thought I understood it. But today I am living it, and feeling the fullness in my heart of knowing that all the bad things that happened to me over the past few weeks have come together to bring a beautiful restoration for our families."

Sam, Katie and Ryan came running over.

"Okay, Alexander. I got Katie and Ryan here so they can hear it too. Are you going to ask my mom to marry you? Are you going to ask to be my dad?"

Alexander's face fell. "I would like nothing more than that, buddy. But I was mean to your mom, and I hurt her. And even though I am so sorry for everything I put her through, it's going to take some time for her to forgive me. But when she does, I promise, not only will I ask her, but I'll have you help me do it, okay?"

Tears sprang to Janie's eyes as she watched her son run to Alexander's arms and hold him tight. How could she have doubted Alexander's love for her?

Yes, he had come here under all sorts of false pretenses. When he pressed her for the truth or facts on issues, instead of lying, he would tell her he couldn't say much. And then there were all the times he had warned her, tried to protect her heart.

He had sacrificed his job for her, the one thing that had mattered most to him in the whole world.

Since that horrible night, Alexander had done everything he could to prove his love for her, and until now, she'd been too blind to see it.

She looked over at Alexander. "I don't need time. The past few days have given me all the time I needed. I'm ready when you are."

Sam tugged on Alexander's pant leg, and Alexander bent down to listen to whatever Sam whispered in his ear.

Alexander grinned, then stepped up to

Janie. He got down on one knee. "Janie, I love you."

Then he looked back at Sam. "What was I supposed to say next?"

Sam groaned and came and stood beside him. "I'll whisper in your ear what you're supposed to say next, okay?"

"Good plan," Alexander said.

Sam whispered, and Alexander spoke. "You're the best woman I've ever known, and I can't imagine spending the rest of my life without you."

Once again, Sam whispered in his ear, and Alexander nodded. Something about the way Alexander was letting her little boy dictate how he got to propose touched her heart in a deeper way than she'd ever thought possible. It was obvious that Alexander didn't just love her, but Sam as well.

"And I love your son, and I want him to be my son. Will you do me the honor of becoming my wife, and letting me become Sam's dad?"

Sam gave a nod and stepped away. But Alexander remained in his position.

"I know this isn't part of the script that Sam gave me, but I also wanted to say that I'm a better man because of you. You've taught me the value of the real things in life, the things that matter most to me. I thought I had my life planned out, but you showed me the life I truly wanted."

Sam groaned. "Enough with the speeches already. You are supposed to give her a ring, she is supposed to take it, and then you are supposed to kiss."

Alexander couldn't help laughing as he stood. "I guess we should have practiced before I got here. I didn't mean to ruin your plans."

He looked over at Janie. "I'm sorry. I don't have a ring. I wasn't that optimistic. I figured at best you would be frosty and polite, and at worst, you'd punch me in the nose, because that's what I deserve. But we can go to Denver and pick out whatever you like."

Janie's dad joined their group. "It might be presumptuous of me, but since Bette died, I've carried her ring around in my pocket. If it's not too weird, I know she'd love for you to have it."

Tears had already been forming in Janie's eyes, but the thought of wearing her mother's ring, the symbol of a marriage she'd always admired and wanted for herself, brought them rolling down her cheeks. More than that, it meant a symbol of her mom would be with her always, and even though she was gone, it felt like she was present for the moment.

As Janie nodded, her father handed the ring to Alexander. Alexander didn't even look at it before offering it to Janie. "Okay. So now I have a ring, which means I've done everything that Sam wants me to do, but the question is what do you want? Would you take this ring and be my wife?"

Janie was crying too hard to do more than hold out her hand, which Alexander seemed to accept as a yes. He slid the ring onto her finger, and at that moment, every broken piece of her heart felt restored.

No, not restored—better than ever. Multiplied beyond her wildest expectations.

Alexander leaned into her and whispered, "I think we're supposed to kiss now, or Sam's going to be mad. Is that okay?"

Janie nodded as he brought his lips to hers, and in his arms, she felt the promise of hope in a future greater than anything they could have planned for themselves—but God had brought all these events of their lives together to make it so.

Epilogue

One year later

The community resource center was booming with activity as Janie entered after picking Sam up from meeting with his reading tutor. Not only had the senator's money funded a grant for the center, but as the new executive director, Alexander had secured several other grants to strengthen the community center and make it a hub of activity for the town's rebuilding efforts.

It had also been enough to give a generous salary to Janie, as well as a couple other full-time staff members, to keep up the work she'd been so afraid they'd have to discontinue.

They'd expanded into an empty storefront next door to have classrooms to help the locals, particularly those whose jobs had been lost as a result of the fire, gain new skills to help them find better employment. They'd even partnered with a college to allow people to take classes online so they could either get or finish their degrees.

Thanks to encouragement from Alexander and her father, Janie would be using that tool as a way to finish her own degree.

She paused at the entrance to Alexander's office. The senator was in there, and it looked like they were having an important meeting, but just as she started to turn away, Alexander waved her in.

As soon as Sam saw the senator, he ran to his arms. "Grandpa!"

It was still weird to see that interaction, but it felt good to know that Sam had some connection to his entire family, that missing piece he'd always longed for. They'd all mutually agreed that now was not the time for Bucky to meet Sam, especially since Bucky still wanted nothing to do with him. But Anne was making up for the lost time of not getting to be a grandmother, and Janie's biggest challenge was not letting the two of them spoil Sam too much.

"The senator was just coming in to tell me that he has dropped his bid for the United States Senate, and when his seat in the Colorado Senate comes up for reelection next year, he won't be running."

The senator nodded. "I lost sight of what's important to me. Between you and Alexander, I realized so much of what I've been missing in life. Because of it, I failed my son. I failed to be a good example, and I failed to see what he'd turned into."

He gave Sam another squeeze. "Our visits to Columbine Springs have shown me the value of working directly with the people, and my dreams of helping others. Anne has me going back to church, and we're going on a mission trip next month."

Sam glared at him. "You're not going to miss my birthday, are you? You've never been to one of my birthdays, and my mom makes the best cake."

The senator smiled and ruffled Sam's hair. "I wouldn't miss it for the world. We leave the day after."

His answer satisfied Sam, who tugged at his hand. "Cool. Are you done talking about grown-up stuff? I just got a new book from my reading teacher, and she said I have to practice reading it to people. Since I'm going to read it to Mom later, we should go read it now."

The senator shrugged as he looked back at Janie and Alexander. "I guess I've been told."

Alexander grinned. "He does think he's the boss around here. I'm not sure what he's going to do when he becomes a big brother and isn't the focus of everyone's lives."

The senator stared directly at Janie's midsection. "You're not expecting already, are you?"

Janie laughed. "No, not yet. We want to wait a while before bringing a baby into the mix."

Then Alexander pulled her into his arms and kissed her. "Now shoo, so I can spend a little quality time with my wife."

The senator chuckled as he let Sam drag him out of the office. She could hear her son chattering down the hall, telling the senator that since he liked Katie so much, he was already asking God for a sister, but Ryan was okay, too, so he wouldn't mind a brother.

When they were finally alone, Alexander closed the door to his office. "Since Jim and Anne are in town, they wanted to take Sam for the evening, and I thought it would be the perfect opportunity to have some quality husband-wife time on our own. What do you think?"

As he gently trailed kisses down her neck, Janie smiled. "You know, just because people tell you we should do things doesn't mean you have to listen. You could have some ideas of your own about our marriage, you know."

Alexander pulled away, then smiled at her. "Why do you think Jim and Anne are here in the first place?"

The look he gave her made her feel warm and loved.

But then he pulled away.

"While I would like to continue this discussion, I did want to show you something else before we got too distracted. William brought me the preliminary drawings for rebuilding your mother's rose garden, and I can't wait to show you what he's come up with."

They'd talked about redoing the rose garden, but with the town still rebuilding, and everyone's funds so tight, Janie had let it take a back burner, as much as she hated to do so. But the love in her husband's eyes reminded her that the things that mattered to Janie were just as important to him.

Once again, Janie thanked God for bringing her the man she needed when she needed him the most. She might joke about how Alexander followed people's ideas about their marriage, especially since he'd practically been forced to propose to her by Sam, but she loved that their relationship was completely about them, and that their love for one another—and his heart—was big enough to include everyone else who cared about them as well.

When he rolled the drawings out on the table, Janie gasped.

"My mom always wanted a fountain in her garden, but my dad always said it was impractical."

"Who said love was supposed to be practical?" Alexander asked, pulling her into his arms again. "Sometimes you have to follow your heart, even if it doesn't make sense."

* * * * *

If you enjoyed this story,
be sure to pick up the
previous book in Danica Favorite's
Double R Legacy miniseries,
The Cowboy's Sacrifice!

Dear Reader,

Living in Colorado high country means that we always face the danger of wildfires. It's amazing how quickly people's lives can change with the simple shift of the wind. My friend Shelley lost her home several years ago in the Hi Meadow fire, and while I didn't know her at that time, our years of friendship have been full of stories of how that fire impacted her family. When I thought about putting a wildfire in my book, I knew that Shelley would be both my inspiration and resource.

I would not be who I am or where I am without the amazing community around me, and I believe that the best way we can all make a difference is by loving and helping those around us. We can all have a positive impact on our world, and it starts with loving our neighbors. You don't have to be rich or powerful to do that. It can be as simple as a shared meal with a friend or a phone call to let them know you care. Your genuine compassion means more to people than you can possibly know.

Let's all spread the love, one person at a time.

Danica Favorite

I love hearing from my readers! Visit my website at DanicaFavorite.com to stay in touch!

Get 4 FREE REWARDS!

We'll send you 2 FREE Books plus 2 FREE Mystery Gifts.

Love Inspired Suspense books showcase how courage and optimism unite in stories of faith and love in the face of danger.

FREE
Value Over
$20

YES! Please send me 2 FREE Love Inspired Suspense novels and my 2 FREE mystery gifts (gifts are worth about $10 retail). After receiving them, if I don't wish to receive any more books, I can return the shipping statement marked "cancel." If I don't cancel, I will receive 6 brand-new novels every month and be billed just $5.24 each for the regular-print edition or $5.99 each for the larger-print edition in the U.S., or $5.74 each for the regular-print edition or $6.24 each for the larger-print edition in Canada. That's a savings of at least 13% off the cover price. It's quite a bargain! Shipping and handling is just 50¢ per book in the U.S. and $1.25 per book in Canada.* I understand that accepting the 2 free books and gifts places me under no obligation to buy anything. I can always return a shipment and cancel at any time. The free books and gifts are mine to keep no matter what I decide.

Choose one: ☐ **Love Inspired Suspense Regular-Print** (153/353 IDN GNWN) ☐ **Love Inspired Suspense Larger-Print** (107/307 IDN GNWN)

Name (please print)

Address   Apt. #

City   State/Province   Zip/Postal Code

Email: Please check this box ☐ if you would like to receive newsletters and promotional emails from Harlequin Enterprises ULC and its affiliates. You can unsubscribe anytime.

Mail to the **Reader Service:**
IN U.S.A.: P.O. Box 1341, Buffalo, NY 14240-8531
IN CANADA: P.O. Box 603, Fort Erie, Ontario L2A 5X3

Want to try 2 free books from another series? Call 1-800-873-8635 or visit www.ReaderService.com.

*Terms and prices subject to change without notice. Prices do not include taxes, which will be charged (if applicable) based on your state or country of residence. Canadian residents will be charged applicable taxes. Offer not valid in Quebec. This offer is limited to one order per household. Books received may not be as shown. Not valid for current subscribers to Love Inspired Suspense books. All orders subject to approval. Credit or debit balances in a customer's account(s) may be offset by any other outstanding balance owed by or to the customer. Please allow 4 to 6 weeks for delivery. Offer available while quantities last.

Your Privacy—Your information is being collected by Harlequin Enterprises ULC, operating as Reader Service. For a complete summary of the information we collect, how we use this information and to whom it is disclosed, please visit our privacy notice located at corporate.harlequin.com/privacy-notice. From time to time we may also exchange your personal information with reputable third parties. If you wish to opt out of this sharing of your personal information, please visit readerservice.com/consumerschoice or call 1-800-873-8635. **Notice to California Residents**—Under California law, you have specific rights to control and access your data. For more information on these rights and how to exercise them, visit corporate.harlequin.com/california-privacy.

LIS20R2

THE WESTERN HEARTS COLLECTION!

19 FREE BOOKS in all!

COWBOYS. RANCHERS. RODEO REBELS.
**Here are their charming love stories in one prized Collection:
51 emotional and heart-filled romances that capture the majesty
and rugged beauty of the American West!**

YES! Please send me **The Western Hearts Collection** in Larger Print. This collection begins with 3 FREE books and 2 FREE gifts in the first shipment. Along with my 3 free books, I'll also get the next 4 books from The Western Hearts Collection, in LARGER PRINT, which I may either return and owe nothing, or keep for the low price of $5.45 U.S./$6.23 CDN each plus $2.99 U.S./$7.49 CDN for shipping and handling per shipment*. If I decide to continue, about once a month for 8 months I will get 6 or 7 more books but will only need to pay for 4. That means 2 or 3 books in every shipment will be FREE! If I decide to keep the entire collection, I'll have paid for only 32 books because 19 books are FREE! I understand that accepting the 3 free books and gifts places me under no obligation to buy anything. I can always return a shipment and cancel at any time. My free books and gifts are mine to keep no matter what I decide.

☐ 270 HCN 5354   ☐ 470 HCN 5354

Name (please print)

Address   Apt. #

City   State/Province   Zip/Postal Code

Mail to the **Reader Service:**
IN U.S.A.: P.O. Box 1341, Buffalo, N.Y. 14240-8531
IN CANADA: P.O. Box 603, Fort Erie, Ontario L2A 5X3

50BWH20